To Vivy, my C.

A Touch of
Templeton

Thankyou so much I would be
lost without you
Love Pauline
xxx

by

P. E Campbell

**Grosvenor House
Publishing Limited**

This book is published by
Grosvenor House Publishing Ltd
28-30 High Street, Guildford, Surrey, GU1 3EL.
www.grosvenorhousepublishing.co.uk

A CIP record for this book
is available from the British Library

ISBN 978-1-78148-941-3

This is for you dad, I miss your wisdom.

Prologue

꙳

A hint of blue forced its way through the night sky, signalling daybreak. If I had done everything right, not strayed off the beaten path, someone else would be standing here instead of me. When I made my decision, I knew there would be consequences, yet I never imagined the price would be so high; I guess you reap what you sow.

"Don't tell me you're shy Patsy, after all your adventurous exploits of this week." The brute's voice was calm as his breath shimmered in the cold night air. It would have been easy to avoid his gaze, disengage from my body, leaving just a shell, void of any feeling or emotion. If I were the same Patsy Cunningham of six days ago, this may have been a viable option, but the woman staring back at this thing, was not the same; no longer content with a twelve-hour day, her only thought centred on working harder from one day to the next. How could I be, after this gut wrenching whirlwind took me to places I never imagined or even dared dream of?

"Do you know what makes the world go round Patsy? Power, power and control," said the animal, trying to take on the persona of a man. Daddy says you only have real power when you have respect, which stems from love, not fear. Oh God, I wish Wallace D Cunningham were standing by my side right now, with his bear-like stature and strong will. I stared hard at my aggressor, daring him to carry out his sick plan, praying that somewhere in that disturbed mind there was a shred of decency, telling him what he was about to do was wrong. Yet, like all bullies, he relished control; got a kick out of hurting people. He moved towards me, I backed away; it seemed all my life I had been backing away, allowing my past to dictate my future. What should I do? Usually I could reason my way out of a problem, analyse, unpick it, find a solution, but there was no logic in what was about to happen to me. I ached with fear; yet, I would die before I gave him the satisfaction of seeing it in my eyes.

"Where's your knight in shining armour? Scuttled away like the coward he is." His words deflected off their intended target, ricocheting into the dark sky. I managed to raise a smile, knowing there was nothing the monster could say or do to change the deep-rooted feelings that had seeped into every orifice of my body; every touch, each moment would stay with me for the rest of my life, even though I was not sure how long that would be. As unbelievable as it sounds, I was happy;

happy that Richard got away; was safe. I could not bear the thought of anything happening to him. He had given me more in the past few days than anyone could. I did not think it was possible to care more for someone than I care for myself, yet, I do. I suppose this is what they call love, real love. Not a word you use now and then to get what you want, but a deep-rooted feeling made up of an intensity that you cannot describe. You only know that you feel more than you have ever felt before and you never want that aching to go away, you want it to stay with you forever.

My body tingled with a mixture of fear and the cold. I closed my eyes imagining Richard's arms around me, keeping me safe and warm; but then the strong grip of the monster returned me to an unsavoury reality, forcing me to the ground. I kept my eyes tightly shut, not wishing to see the face of pure evil. Then suddenly a voice coming from no-where screamed, *Stand your ground, don't let him win...fight, fight.* I could not work out where it was coming from, and then I realised, it was me, but not as I was now, but a young girl of twelve years old, buried for so long I had forgotten she ever existed. I could hear her clearly in my mind, shaking me, pushing me to fight, sounding so different to how I remember, no longer frightened or tormented, but strong, powerful. "Why are you here?" I ask, "What do you want?"

Don't let him win...don't let him win, she replies. Then she is gone in whisper. As I felt the force of the body on top of me, I knew at that moment, the animal was right. No hero would be coming to my rescue; I was on my own. I opened my eyes, deciding to face my terror head on; no longer submissive or weak.

I deny you, refuse to accept this defilement, refuse to let you win, If I go, I go my way not yours, I will use every ounce of the essence remaining within me to destroy any sordid plans you have for me. So, come on you bastard, take a chance if you dare, because I am ready for you.

Chapter 1

ॐ

Six days ago – Monday

It was unusual for me to be on the bus so late. I was usually the first one in and the last one out, but having worked into the early hours of Sunday morning, I could not ignore my body's demand for rest. Mr Rawlings says he has never met anyone that works as hard as I do. He says it like it is a bad thing; what is wrong with being passionate about your work? Me, I eat, sleep and dream the law. I figure if you are good at something you should work at it, make yourself invincible, irreplaceable, that way people value you; you are worth something. I have never understood why people spend so much time on things they are not good at. I'm perfectly happy with my nose stuck in a law book for most of my waking hours. I do not do social. I mean, I feel uncomfortable around people away from work. I have one precious gem of a friend, Anna, and she is more than enough for me. I can be myself around her, because she knows what I have been through, which makes my life a whole lot easier.

"How are we doing for room up there, Miss Sharp?" The teacher shouted from the bottom deck.

"We're ok, send them up." Gaggles of children began filing onto the top deck "That's it, go to the back and sit down, quiet please. Gabriel you sit here next to this nice lady."

Gabriel stared at the unoccupied seat next to me with dark blue eyes and unruly hair tucked under a blue anorak, and then hiked his way up, fiddling around until he was comfortable, with his fresh face beaming of innocence. I mustered a smile before turning away and looking out the window.

I suppose it would have been nice to say hello or something, make playful conversation with the bright-eyed little boy, but my nature was not equipped for such frivolities. Anyway, I doubt me droning on about a lost weekend stuck behind a laptop unravelling the pros and cons on the law of Council enforcement would have set him up for the day.

"I want to sit next to Gabriel." A young blond boy stood in front of me.

"There's no room, come and sit with me" said the young teacher, grabbing the little boy and planting him squarely on her lap.

"No, I want to sit with Gabriel," the child protested, twisting and squirming in her arms. The whimper rippled into an agonising scream, the child seemed determined to get his way, yet throughout Gabriel remained calm and surprisingly unperturbed by his needy friend, who clearly could not survive without him. So there I was faced with a dilemma on a wet and windy Monday morning, should I grant the spoilt little brat what he wanted, thereby giving him the false impression that in life all you have to do is throw a tantrum to get what you want, or should I stay firm, teaching him the valuable lesson of self-control.

"It's alright; let him sit next to Gabriel." I finally relented, giving up my comfortable seat by the window.

"Thank you" said a very relieved young woman as peace was restored.

"No problem, call it my good deed for the day." I replied, making my way downstairs as the ungrateful little boy scrambled into my seat, without a thank you. Maybe I was getting soft, at the ripe old age of twenty-eight, a luxury I could ill afford in a cutthroat world where's it's killed or be killed.

"Morning, one and all! And how are we on this wonderful wet and windy day?" I received various grunts and murmurs from my team of lawyers, who, like me, had various deadlines to hit, most of which were yesterday.

I found a post-it note stamped on the front of my computer. *Patsy, pop in and see me when you get in.* Mr Rawlings my line manager had a way of catching

3

me before I started my day with a shopping list of things for me to do, which usually required me doing more and him doing less.

"Ah Patsy, nice weekend?" said Mr Rawlings as he nursed his tea.

"Fine thanks." I lied having spent the whole weekend working on the Hastings Brief; a difficult document that was taking forever to finish.

"Ah, the Hastings File." Mr Rawlings said, delving through his desk in a feeble attempt to look busy. "I've received an additional request for information relating to the final brief. I understand that this will involve slightly more research but we need to confirm the position in respect of the public interest aspect and possible challenges."

"I thought we had already agreed the public interest aspect was not a relevant factor and we should focus on the pros and cons of the legislation." I said, hoping Mr Rawlings would grow a pair and tell the powers-that-be to leave lawyering to the lawyers for once.

"Noted, but I was speaking to Henry Castle in the press office and he raised concerns that this aspect was not being considered." It never ceased to amaze me how easy it was for Mr Rawlings to develop amnesia. "In fact, concerns were raised that his team had not been included in the process."

It was my time to come out fighting. I liked fighting. I was good at it. "With all due respect I have a list of all the departments that you wanted involved and they were not on it." There was no respect whatsoever. I knew it and so did he.

"Well I think it's important that they get on board. Here's a list of the additional points I need you to consider," said Rawlings asserting his position.

"Fine, but I require a written note confirming you have requested the additional information as well as confirmation that you instructed me to include the press in the process."

Rawlings opened a file without looking up, his way of dismissing me, but I was going no-where until he acknowledged me, finally he obliged. "I don't think that will be necessary."

"I seem to remember that the client department has never seen eye-to-eye with the press on this issue, and that was your reason for excluding them in the first place. If you have a problem recollecting that discussion I have a copy of the e-mail you sent in relation to that particular point, which may help to jog your memory, Mr Rawlings."

"I don't think it's absolutely essential, but if you insist."

"I do."

"Well I'll get it over to you now."

"Thank you Mr Rawlings."

My golden rule is, always cover your back; because when things go wrong, people invariably look for someone to blame. Mud sticks and I had no intention of it sticking to me.

On winning the battle but not the war, I returned to my desk, securing my coat on the back of my chair, cursing as I saw countless e-mails. I suppose a caffeine boost would have provided a perfect kick-start to my day, but I am not a coffee person. I love the smell but hate the taste.

I peruse the Hastings file, which, in spite of Rawlings' additional demands, I was determined to finish by the end of the day. It had been a thorn in my side for a week and I wanted it gone.

"Morning Miss Cunningham." Tina, my newly qualified lawyer, was standing over me looking nervous.

"Tina, I'm your manager not your mother, its Patsy." I loved Tina. She says every word in a whisper. Shame I'll have shatter the illusion and toughen her up. Unfortunately, this is a prerequisite in an unforgiving world, because when you are standing on your feet faced with a despicable opponent and an even more despicable judge, you've got to have your wits about you, and no matter how frightened you may be, you can never show any fear.

"Sorry Patsy. Melanie's called in sick today."

"And that's my problem how?"

"The Jordan case is listed at Mabley Magistrates, and I can't go because I'm doing a Pre-Trial Review at Inner London."

"Mike!" I shouted to the other end of the office.

"Sorry, no can do, I'm preparing a bundle that has to be couriered over by twelve today."

"I've already asked," said Tina

"Did Melanie say what was wrong with her?"

"No."

"She'll have a pretty good idea when I get hold of her. I do not believe this! Clearly it's too late to farm it out to a barrister." Tina nodded in agreement. "Then it looks like I've won first prize doesn't it, that's all I need." I noticed that Tina was close to tears and I suddenly felt guilty for taking my frustration out on an innocent bystander.

"Eh what's going on here? I'm sorry if I've been barking this morning but quiet and serene doesn't quite work for me."

"It's not that, it's just that this is my first hearing without you there to hold my hand, and I've really been working myself up about it. What if I do something wrong?" I pulled Melanie's empty chair next to me and beckon Tina to sit down.

"Tina, what you're feeling is completely normal. To be honest, I would be worried if you weren't nervous. Now what is the golden rule?"

"Preparation is the key."

"And are you prepared?"

"I think so … Yes, I am prepared. We just have to go through disclosure schedules and the agreed date for service of witness statements."

"Be careful with disclosure. Focus on the key issues. Don't agree to disclose irrelevant evidence; remember anything between the clients and us is privileged, they have no right to see it; don't get trapped into a fishing expedition. If they ask for anything outside the period in question, what do you do?"

"I advise the court that I wish to raise concerns in relation to its admissibility and the erroneous nature of the application."

"Good girl! Never agree to anything until you've had a chance to go through it with a fine tooth comb."

"Yes ... Patsy."

"You've got my mobile, call me at any time; I don't care how little the problem may be, talk to me. Be polite, but firm; because once they see any sign of weakness they'll be all over you."

"Thank you Patsy."

"Never worry about nerves. The most seasoned lawyer gets nervous when standing to his/her feet. You, my dear, are a cool, confident woman and I have complete faith in your ability. I know you will not let me down. Now bugger off, I've got Melanie's arse to cover."

I watch as Tina makes her way back to her desk, packing her case for court. God it's hard to believe that I was ever that green. I am very glad that I am at the beginning of Tina's journey, in a profession dominated by men, who view the women in it as nothing more than gate crashers with a limited shelf-life. I wish I could shield her from having to face her first lost case, difficult and argumentative clients, refusing to take advice and then blaming her when it all goes wrong. The callous, arrogant Judges, who relish humiliating you in open court, the sleepless nights leading up to trial, wondering, fretting as she asks herself, 'what have I missed?'

However, her biggest judgment call will be the day she looks into her babies eyes for the first time, that tiny person wielding their own agenda; will she be happy with her choice? Is any woman? Maybe she will be one of the lucky ones and have it all.

Chapter 2

꒰ꕤ꒱

"Patsy Cunningham, this is indeed an honour, what the bloody hell are you doing here?" said my favourite environmental health officer, Denise Simpson.

"How you doing Denise, good to see you! It's been ages." I greeted Denise with a hug and was genuinely pleased to see her. She was one of those clients who was passionate about her work, which meant she did everything right.

"I was expecting Melanie," said Denise.

"Mel's not feeling too good today, so you've got me."

"Well I'm glad it's you and congratulations on your promotion. Well deserved! The only down side is, I don't get to see that much of you anymore."

"Doesn't stop you ringing me every five minutes though, does it?"

"Come on, at least give me time to wean myself off you!"

"You are so full it ... Okay, I've had a chance to read through the file and I have a good idea of what's going on. Have you heard from Mr Jordan?"

"Not a dicky bird. Is he represented?" asked Denise.

"There's nothing here." I trudged through the file, praying I had not missed anything. "He didn't turn up for his interview under caution, so we don't have any idea which way he intends to go, but judging by the evidence I'm sure we can secure a guilty plea today." I continued with an air of confidence.

"He's banged to rights Pats, you've seen the photographs?" Denise ruffled in her bag and found her glasses, which she quickly put on.

"Yep" I respond continuing to flick through the file.

"The restaurant is slap bang in the middle of Castle Row, the best street in the area. It's strange though, we've carried out regular yearly inspections and there was never any trace of an infestation before, but this time round it was so bad we had no choice but to close the place down."

"It says here we received complaints?"

"One complaint: an anonymous caller."

"Can I see the current inspection notices?" My legal head was now firmly in place as Denise searched through the paperwork contained within a large folder. I am surprised to see that the restaurant is in pristine condition. "You sure this is the same place? It looks beautiful." I continued to look through the notices and attached photographs. "If I wasn't prosecuting him, I'd eat there myself."

"Believe me Pats, you couldn't afford it." Denise whispered.

"How much did this lot cost?"

"Don't ask, but the place is immaculate now. He sacked his manager and is running the place with his wife until he finds a replacement. Do you think that will give us problems in securing a conviction?" Denise looked a little worried.

"Not at all, it doesn't change the fact that the breach occurred and it was serious enough for you to shut him down. This only goes to mitigating circumstances. I'm confident that we can secure a conviction and you know me, I always get my man." I came across as a little arrogant, but it was true. I had an unblemished record and had secured more guilty pleas first time up than any other lawyer and there was no harm in being proud of the fact.

"Good, let's make an example of him," replied Denise confidence restored.

"As usual we're on the same page. Let's see if we can find out what's happening." Denise and I made our way into court five. Solicitors mulled around the usher, trying to get their cases heard first, because no lawyer wants to be stuck in court all day. I told Denise to take a seat at the back and, not one to stand on ceremony, hustled my way through towards a flustered usher trying desperately to keep track of all the names, being thrust at her from all directions."

"Wait a minute I can only take one name at a time. Hello Miss Cunningham, ain't seen you for a while."

"Hi Lucy, still keeping you busy I see." I jumped in, ignoring the other lawyers' looks of disapproval.

"Why don't we see you anymore? That new lawyer's always so serious."

"Don't worry I'm working on her. How are your amateur dramatics going?" I asked.

"We start *Sweet Charity* next week. I have a massive role, but I think I can pull it off, or at least die trying." Said Lucy, whose large personality and upbeat manner was always refreshing. People assume that the most powerful person in a courtroom is the Judge, How wrong they are! It is definitely that individual, who gets you out of court, as soon as possible and when they are genuinely nice; it makes all our lives a lot easier. Ushers are like hard working lawyers; unappreciated and doing far too much for far too little.

"I'm on the Jordan case."

"Oh it's you!" said Lucy.

"That sounds ominous. Is there a problem?"

"Mr Jordan is here ... with his legal representative," Lucy murmured under her breath, as if afraid that someone would overhear her. "A Mr Templeton."

"Alright so where is this Mr Templeton?" Sometimes life has a way of throwing you a curve ball, causing you to lose your footing by taking you to a place that leaves you uncertain and unsure. It was an unwelcome feeling because I hate anything I cannot understand. "Let's go outside shall we, it's a little busy in here isn't it?" said the tall man gently taking my arm as he escorted me outside. I could see Denise looking over, so I nodded, indicating that her presence was not required. The man looked out of place amongst the shabbily dressed lawyers in his immaculate dark blue suit and sharp yellow tie.

"Where's your client?" I asked carefully removing my arm.

Mr Templeton pointed to a small man sitting patiently in a row of seats at the end of the large court corridor. I could see how nervous Mr Jordan looked and wanted to kick myself for feeling a little sorry for him.

"We haven't been formally introduced. My name is Richard Templeton from Templeton and Rye Chambers. Mr Jordan has been a client of mine for some time."

I lived by rules, they governed every hour of my waking day, rules keep you on the straight and narrow, focused on your goal. When I walk into a room facing my adversary I look them straight in the eye and stare them down. This gives me immediate control and leaves no room for doubt that I intended to wipe the floor with them, hence my unblemished record. Therefore, I instinctively knew something was wrong when I found myself looking everywhere except into Richard Templeton's piercing blue eyes, which seemed to exude an intensity the likes of which I had never experienced, making me uncomfortable, disorientated. Yet, I had a client in the other room expecting results and I did not intend to let her down for the sake of some misguided, inexplicable emotion that I neither wanted nor understood.

"Sorry I haven't come across your Chambers before, do you specialise in criminal law?"

"I've dabbled in it from time to time but this is more in line with Environmental Health, with which I am very familiar. I'm sorry I don't think I got your name."

"Patsy Cunningham. Senior Lawyer for Bramford City Council" God I sound like a newsreader.

"I was expecting a Melanie Bentley?"

"Oh she's sick, I mean she's off work today," I resented Melanie more and more for landing me in it.

"I hope it's nothing serious. In any event, her loss appears to be my gain," I do not like compliments. I never know how to react, I over analyse them believing there is always an ulterior motive behind them. Therefore, my response can only be one of attack.

"We are ready to proceed, do we have any indications as to your clients plea. Bearing the evidential facts in mind, I am assuming your client is leaning towards a guilty plea?" I was on autopilot.

"You do get down to brass-tacks don't you?"

"Well that's what we're here for. Time is money and I'm sure your time is a lot more costly than mine."

Mr Templeton once again took my arm and led me to an empty area in the corner of the corridor. I once again pulled away only to be confronted with a heavenly sweet-smelling hint of cologne.

"It may have escaped your notice but I am capable of walking without your assistance Mr Templeton."

"Sorry, it's instinctive for me to take a woman's arm."

"Although that may be quite gallant, it's not something I'm used to, so if you could refrain from doing so in the future I'd be..."

"You're very direct, aren't you Miss Cunningham?"

"Yes, Mr Templeton, because that's just the kind of girl I am." Mr Templeton slightly lowered his head towards mine almost brushing me with his lips.

"Surely, 'woman' would be a more apt description in your case, don't you think?" Who is this man, where did he come from?

"Mr Templeton..."

"Please, call me Richard."

"I will stick to Mr Templeton, if that's alright with you." I felt like a rat backed into a corner. Richard Templeton took a deep breath as if trying to collect his thoughts and I felt triumphant that I had managed to belay his attempts at charming me into some sort of submission. I had to keep my wits about me; this wall was made of granite and I was not about to let anyone break it down. Being Patsy Cunningham meant doing exactly what it said on the tin, say it as it is, with no chinks in her armour.

"I have advised my client to ask for an adjournment today." He said calmly.

"On what basis?"

"I intend to make written representations ... on the other hand if we could have a brief case conference with your client and my client today, we may be able to arrive at an amicable solution."

"Listen Mr Templeton, there are only two options available to your client, either he enters a guilty plea at which point he will be sentenced today, or he enters a not guilty plea and the matter goes for trial."

"You've neglected to mention the third option of the adjournment."

"I will be opposing any application for an adjournment on the basis that Mr Jordan failed to attend an interview under caution and has had ample opportunity to seek legal representation."

"Unfortunately my client was out of the country at the time the letters requesting he attend an interview were sent. I have evidence with me supporting this, which I did intend to make part of the written representations. I am sure you are aware, Miss Cunningham, the law entitles everyone to present his or her side of the story. Reputation is everything in my client's line of business. He has worked hard to establish himself and a conviction could ruin him, put an end to his livelihood.

Besides, due to my client's absence, I have only just received legal instructions."

"You've already admitted that Mr Jordan has been a client of yours for some time, so there is no reason to justify any postponement. Come on Mr Templeton this is a delay tactic and you know it, your client is banged to rights."

"That's your opinion Miss Cunningham and you are entitled to it. In any event, I am sure you have had sight of the extensive works carried out to remedy the breach, and are aware that those responsible have been dismissed. In addition, your own client's witness statement confirms at least three annual visits have taken place previously, where no traces of infestation were located at the premises. All these add up to strong mitigating circumstances. My client has no previous convictions, so any penalty imposed is likely to be nominal." I knew he was right and hated the fact.

"Patsy, is everything alright?" Denise had always been impatient; I did not want her anywhere near. True to form, Mr Templeton extended his hand with style and grace and she of course responded accordingly.

"Hello, Richard Templeton."

"Denise Simpson." Templeton wasted no time in making the most of the opportunity, immediately calling Mr Jordan over where he made introductions all round. It was unusual for me to be in this position, as I am used to being in control, but from the moment, I met this man he had methodically taken a hold of everything I wanted to say and do.

"We were just discussing…"

"There's no need for you to tell my client what we were discussing Mr Templeton, seeing as no decision has been reached as yet." He ignored my concerns and homed in on Denise.

"As I was saying to Miss Cunningham, surely there's no harm in discussing a way forward. I'm seeking to make written representations, but if there's a way we could dispose of this matter today, then I would be happy to speak to the usher and request that the case be set back to allow parties a little more time."

"You will do nothing of the kind Mr Templeton." I tried my best not to raise my voice.

"Patsy, maybe Mr Templeton's has a point, surely there's no harm in considering all the options is there?" This cannot be happening.

"Denise can I see you for a moment?" Denise could tell by the way that I almost yanked her arm out of its socket that she was about to be scolded. Mr Templeton watched me intensely whilst I took Denise through the large double doors out of his view.

"Whatever happened to 'we want to make an example of him'? I thought we were on the same page here. Den, you have a strong case, do not settle for less. I can read this Templeton like a book; he's going for a caution!"

"And would that be so bad, I mean he doesn't have any priors and Pats, look at him ... Mr Jordan I mean, he looks terrified! I can't help feeling a little sorry for him." This morning I had an airtight case, now it was slipping through my fingers. If I remained focused, maybe just maybe, I could salvage something from this.

"Sorry to interrupt but I thought it best to speak to the usher, who has kindly agreed to set our case back on the list, we've got about half an hour. I've managed to secure a room. I'll lead the way shall I?" Richard Templeton interrupted, as he gently led Denise away.

Chapter 3

꙰

Richard Templeton observed as Patsy ran across the road, dragging her small pulley case filled with files, Denise by her side. He waited for her to look back, and was surprised and disappointed when she did not. She had fought him every step of the way, but each word and gesture between them stimulated him, pushing him to press her buttons just so that he could keep feeling the sensations she seemed to draw from him. Patsy was strong and resilient, yet he noticed she avoided any eye contact, looking everywhere except directly at him, which showed a vulnerability, a shyness that left him needing to find out more. He remembered how she gently took Aalie Jordan's hand at the bottom of the court steps, telling him she was glad they had reached agreement, whilst warning him what the consequences of any further misdemeanours would mean. But as she wished his friend well, he knew she meant it. There was warmth in her voice and, for a spilt second, a hint of a smile.

* * *

"A formidable young woman, if we had been in there much longer she would have had the shirt off my back I think," said Aalie Jordan to a pre-occupied Richard.

"Yes, I dare say she would," Replied Richard still a little dazed.

"Well once again I am indebted to you my friend."

"With you Aalie it's always a pleasure, never a chore. I was pleased to help." Richard's words were greeted with a hearty hug from his favourite and most trusted client.

"What happens now?"

"Miss Simpson will prepare the caution, you sign and that will be the end of it, unless…"

"There will be no unless Richard." A large car pulls up and a smartly dressed chauffeur gets out, opening the back passenger door, "Can I give you a lift?"

"No, I have to get back to Chambers and it's quicker by train. I'll be in touch."

"Yes, and Richard, would you consider taking advice from a less learned but wise old man." Richard nods "Try working a little less and enjoying life a little more."

Chapter 4

I wanted to scream at the injustice of it, outwitted in my own backyard by a man merely passing through. Not only did he get Denise to agree to a caution, it was all I could do to convince her to demand her costs for the investigation. She was smitten by Templeton the Great, would have streaked in the dock at his say so. It did not help that the main topic of conversation all the way back was Richard this, Richard that. I smiled in the right places, and would be the last to deny that the look of relief on Mr Jordan's face did not exactly fill me with trepidation. Yet, I hated losing, walking away with less than expected. Why is it that all your achievements sink into insignificance with one failure? If I ever see that man, again it will be too soon.

"Patsy there's a lady on the phone from Templeton and Rye." I was beginning to forget what my life was like before he was in it.

"I'm not here."

"But I've already told her I've seen you coming in." Mike waved the phone in my direction not even bothering to recognise how worked up I was.

"Then tell her you saw me going out again."

"I can't do that!"

"Well tell them what you like, I'm taking the Hastings file and working from home this afternoon."

I suppose I was acting like a petulant child, throwing my toys out of the pram because I did not get my way, strangely mirroring the behaviour of the child I had ridiculed just a few hours earlier. It's probably poetic justice that my advice to Tina had come back to bite me square on the arse because, the fact is, I simply was not prepared for the likes of Richard Templeton, with his swagger and calm demeanour accompanied by his impeccable taste in clothes and matching looks. How dare he come into my territory and disjoint me this way?

"You off?" Mike asked as I packed the bits and pieces hastily in an attempt to get out of the office as quickly as possible.

"Oh yes." I try to ignore Mike as I throw the papers into my trusted pulley that I am not looking forward to lugging home.

"Everything alright?" Mike appeared sympathetic as he helped me close the heavy case.

"Everything's fine Mike. Sometimes I take myself a little too seriously, that's all."

"The woman from Templeton & Rye said they'd call back later."

"That'll be nice for her." I grab my coat, having no desire to share my frustrations, but Mike's was un-phased.

"You weren't dealing with them in court today were you? It's just that I always thought they only dealt with large commercial stuff, big mergers, that sort of thing."

"Well maybe they're diversifying."

"Who were you dealing with?"

"I don't know; someone called Richard Templeton."

"Not, the Richard Templeton?"

"Yes, 'the' Richard Templeton, unless there's more than one." Mike rushed over to his computer and started clicking away.

"This is the guy you were dealing with today?" I made my way over to Mike's computer and reluctantly looked at the face of Richard Templeton, smugly staring back at me. The picture did him no justice.

"Yeah and ... what of it?"

"Patsy, this guy is a legend! He won his first big case at just twenty-five, secured damages for his client of four hundred and fifty grand. What was the name of your case again?"

"Mike I really don't have time for this."

"Jordan right ... yes I knew it." Mike ignored me, frantically tapping away, "Here, Aalie Jordan and Malik Tazim; that was his first big case, the one that put him on the map. Mr Jordan was his first big client, no wonder he was representing him today. I would have paid money to see him at Mabley." Mike continued reading:

"Richard Templeton, co-partner of Templeton and Rye, ranked in the top five set of Chambers ... shit, he won barrister of the year two years running for his commercial International work. At thirty-two, he holds a senior position in Templeton and Rye ..." Jesus, he must be minted. I'd sell my soul to get just one foot in that door."

"I'll see you tomorrow Mike, you've got my number if you need me."

"What shall I tell Templeton's when they call back? Shall I give them your number?"

"No, put them through to Mr Rawlings. I'm sure he'll be only too pleased to speak to them."

Like everyone, I had encountered today, Mike was in awe of this man, who had swept into my life like a tidal wave, disrupting, tainting everything around me. Mike shovelled information down my throat that I neither wanted nor needed. Maybe I was being unreasonable but that was my prerogative. Something had happened to me, like a trigger going off in my head, but instead of feeling excitement, there was fear. I knew something was coming but I would do anything to avoid whatever that was. I prayed that by tomorrow the events of today and these strange unwanted feelings would be a distant memory. Tonight I was determined to ensure my evening would only consist of two things, the Hastings file and a large tub of Ben and Jerry's.

Chapter 5

❧

Richard Templeton listened to the intercom to signal that his secretary had placed his call.

"Sorry Mr Templeton but Miss Cunningham has left the office for the afternoon." An efficient voice stated.

"I thought she just got back."

"Apparently the young man was mistaken. Would you like me to find out if she can be contacted on another number?"

"No ... Maggie can you come in for a moment and bring the diary."

Richard Templeton took solace in the fact that he lived a life without complications, with everything in its proper place, just as it should be, where he knew the right people, mixing within a social circle of the elite and privileged. Yet, for the first time in his straightforward existence, he wondered what it would be like to step out of that comfortable box, where every cog sat perfectly in place and turned in sync with one another. Why had this young woman made such an impression on him, why was it so difficult for him to get her out of his mind? In a way, he was glad when she refused to take his call. It probably would be best to allow the spark that had ignited between them to fizzle out, die away, because all it could lead to was a world of trouble.

* * *

Maggie Anderson entered Richard's office and made herself comfortable in the familiar surroundings. With her greying hair tied tightly in a crisp bun, white cotton blouse and navy blue skirt, she had earned pole position among his strong administrative team.

"How did it go today?" asked Maggie.

"As well as could be expected," Richard sat back in his chair thinking. "What have I got on this week?"

"There's the case conference with Wilmington's at two and I've pencilled you in with Hammond for four thirty." Maggie flicked through the pages of the small book, which rested on the lap of her crossed legs.

"I'd forgotten about that."

"I could re-schedule."

"No, better keep it in. What about tomorrow?"

"Busy, busy I'm afraid. There's the case management conference at the High Court listed for ten, which invariably means eleven, followed by another case conference with Alders."

"It's never ending," said Richard.

"I could ask Kingsley to take it; he's been chomping at the bit to get his teeth into a juicy case, and his three day trial went down last week. Oh by the way, Jonathan Southern came to see you this morning."

"Jonathan, but isn't he penned in for Thursday?"

"That's what I told him, but he was very insistent."

"What on earth for?"

"He wouldn't say, he appeared quite agitated, waited nearly an hour before storming off."

"That's not like Jonathan."

There was a knock on the door. "Sorry to interrupt Mr Templeton but someone appears to have left this package outside your office," said the young girl who slowly entered the room under the watchful eye of Maggie, the girl handed over the package accompanied by a lingering smile in Richard's direction.

"Thank you Hannah … that will be all."

"Yes Miss Anderson," Hannah retreated.

Richard watched as Hannah expertly manoeuvred out of his office, taking just long enough to ensure she was noticed. "Nice girl."

"Mm" Maggie was not impressed by the Hannah's flirtatious manner and tight skirt above the knee, as she made a note in her diary simply entitled 'dress code.'

Richard examined the large brown envelope. "It's addressed to Jonathan."

"He must have forgotten it." Maggie replied, taking it from Richard, inspecting it.

"Better give him a call and let him know we have it."

"Will do, anything else?"

"Yes I would love a coffee."

"I second that" Rupert Rye, Richard's partner, entered the office not bothering to knock. "Morning Maggie" Like Richard, Rupert was tailored with precision; wearing a dark suit with a daring burgundy tie.

"Surely it's closer to the afternoon, wouldn't you say?" Maggie responded raising a little smile.

"Now, now Maggie, I refuse to be scolded, on account of working flat-out covering your boss's unexplained absence all morning."

"Thank you Maggie," said Richard as Maggie left, but not before straightening her slightly rumpled skirt.

Rupert browsed through some discarded law books resting on Richard's desk. "Where have you been all morning?"

"I've been in court." Richard turned his chair towards the large bay window. Rupert sat on the small sofa observing his partner who was miles away. It seemed like only yesterday, that he had taken this bright, young unseasoned barrister under his wing after Richard turned to him for help during his first big case. He remembered how Richard fought to fend off the efforts of his more experienced colleagues to take the reins, as well as the glory; and how he would leave Richard in Chambers late into the night and find him there first thing in the morning. He loved Richard's hunger to succeed, his belief in himself, which had no hint of arrogance. Therefore, it was only right that when Rupert decided it was time to set up his own practice he took Richard with him.

"I didn't know any of your cases were up today."

"I wasn't in the High Court. I was in Mabley Magistrates Court in Bramfield."

"What in God's name were you doing there?"

"You remember Mr Jordan?"

"Yes of course, your first big runner."

"Well he got into a spot of bother with the local council and he asked for my help."

"Surely one of your hungry pupils could have taken care of it."

"This was personal. I would not have trusted it to anyone else. His livelihood was at stake."

"As serious as all that?"

"Yes, as serious as all that."

"Never get on the wrong side of the local authority; they're more powerful than God. Well did you win?"

"Of sorts, got away with a caution."

"Then why the glum face?"

"A very skilful local solicitor managed to wheedle costs out of me."

"On a caution, is that ethical?"

"Probably not, but she knew that my client would have sold his soul to avoid a conviction and took full advantage of it."

"How much did she get?"

"The lot, the lady was not for turning." Richard smiled, thinking back to his earlier run-in with Patsy.

"Alright, what was she a blond or brunette?"

"She was, in fact, quite stunning. She had spirit, fight and I can honestly say, is by far the most obstinate woman I have ever met."

"You sound smitten, how about a spot of lunch, you can tell me all about her?"

"No ... thanks, but I have a few calls to make."

Maggie entered carrying two cups of coffee on a tray, Rupert took his cup "Thank you Maggie, I shall take my coffee and withdraw. Are you sure I can't twist your arm Richard?"

"I'll take a rain check. Maggie did you manage to get hold of Jonathan?"

"I tried calling his office and his mobile but there's no answer,"

"Alright, lock it away in the safe for now and keep trying. I'm sure he will re-trace his steps and realise he's left it here. Maggie I've been thinking; maybe it would be a good idea to farm out the Alders case to Kingsley. See how he's fixed for tomorrow afternoon and leave my diary free and can you get Bramfield City Council back, see if we can get another number for Miss Cunningham."

Chapter 6

❧

Tuesday

Last night I dreamt I was back in that room, frightened and alone, being held against my will by a deluded, sick individual who blamed me for everything that was wrong in his life. I had not thought about Samuel Meadows in a long time. Yet, when I least expect it he re-appears, an unwelcome guest in my life. I hate the fact that he is still part of me, but thankfully, he no longer takes hold the way he used to. It's funny how fear becomes a part of you, how you carry it around with you, until you cannot imagine your life without it. But, thankfully, I am a lot stronger now and my wall of granite keeps me safe. At least I managed to complete the Hastings briefing and was able to draft a detailed document to the client, including the dreaded public interest aspect, so that was one less thing for me to do. Ben and Jerry's also helped to soften the blow.

Maybe it was the fact that the sun was beaming through the office window; indicating that it was going to be a beautiful day that gave me the kick I needed to put the whole Richard Templeton thing into perspective. How could I have thought for one second that there was even the remote possibility that someone like that would ... God just thinking about it sounds completely stupid. I am not pretty or even sexy. I've spent my life envying those animals that can hide away and hibernate, cutting themselves off for months at a time in a safe warm environment. For me, the world is not safe, or warm, it's cold and unforgiving. I expect that it is what I love about the law; it's methodical, practical free. You have a problem, you solve it, find a solution, if only life were that simple.

"Morning Patsy, my hearing went really well! The trial's listed for September." Tina seemed significantly more relaxed than yesterday.

"Good girl, I knew you wouldn't let me down and now that you've got the first one out of the way your confidence will grow."

"Yeah, the defence were a bit stroppy but I handled them just like you said, I showed no fear. How did the Jordan case go?"

"I've had better days, but hey, the client's happy and that's all that matters." Another rule I live by is never take your problems into work.

"Has anyone heard from Melanie?"

"She sent in a sick note for the week." I would have happily throttled Melanie had she been in front of me at that moment, but I was sure that by her return, I would have calmed down.

My phone rang. I hesitated before picking it up but then grabbed the receiver.

"Hello Patsy Cunningham, legal services"

"Oh, so you're still alive then?"

"Anna!"

"It's nice to know you remember my name, what happened to you? We were supposed to hook up this weekend. I tried calling, where were you?"

"I am so sorry! I got bogged down with work."

"Now why doesn't that surprise me? Pats you are something else."

"I have no excuse. I am the worst best friend ever."

"You'll get no arguments from me. The question is, what are you going to do to make it up to me?"

I tried to make amends. "This weekend, I promise we'll spend the day together."

"No can do, I'm working." Anna replied.

"We'll sort something out, I promise, promise, promise. Anyway, what you been up to?"

"Well, I spent most of my Saturday morning wrestling a group of very determined women to the ground in that warehouse sale in Bond Street you were supposed to accompany me to."

"Were you successful in your endeavours?"

"A pair of Jimmy Choo's is lying safely in a box at the bottom of my wardrobe as we speak, I won't be able to eat for a month but it was worth it. I miss you, when are you going to escape that evil place where they keep your pay-check and spend some time with your long suffering and neglected friend."

Anna and I had been comrades-in-arms since school, forging an unusual friendship created through a common enemy, fear, which manifested through the blind hatred of a group of our peers who travelled in packs, too cowardly to strike alone. Anna stood by me when no one else would. She was a sounding board, helping me through those school gates every morning to face the name-calling, physical abuse and exclusion. Even when they were at their worst, she never left my side.

Anna Myers was one of the few people I knew who felt comfortable in her own skin. She revelled in defying strict rules, chiselling herself into a defiant adolescent, ignoring her well-to-do parents and teachers, all demanding she conform.

I, on the other hand, adopted a different approach, immersing myself into the Emily Bronte's and Jane Austin's, which transported me into a make-believe world, consisting of broad shouldered men and happy endings. I threw myself into endeavours providing rewards in the form of school prizes and accolades from my parents and teachers, yet Anna never resented me, because she understood this was my way of coping.

Over the years, we have grown closer, bound together by secret memories.

I was not surprised when Anna bagged a job as a beauty consultant in one of the more exclusive department stores, working her magic on countless affluent shoppers. Even as a child, she lived and breathed magazines, escaping to a world where there was only room for perfect skin and elegantly moulded bodies. Never tiring of preaching to me and anyone else who would listen, that with all the products in the world, there was no reason for a woman to look bad. She frequently made her point by transforming me into her own life-size mannequin, a process which subjected me to foundations that cooled my dark brown skin, eye shadows accentuating what Anna described as my deep brown eyes, along with lip-glosses ranging from soft purples to deep reds.

I recall it taking her months to persuade me to cut my hair, bombarding me with one magazine after another, whilst banging home that only certain faces can carry a short cut and I was one of them. When I finally relented and watched the skilful hand of Anna's trusted hairdresser, pull and snip away I felt sick and even cried. However, as usual Anna was right, my short Halle Berry cut with a hint of light brown colour against my jet-black hair actually looked quite nice and now, I love my short, crisp look, which Anna describes as "sassy."

On the odd occasion that she managed to persuade me to venture out, I would prepare for an interrogation where I was required to provide intricate details of the outfit being selected, *Dress shabbily and they remember the dress; dress impeccably and they remember the woman,* one of the many quotes taken from Anna's heroine and inspiration Co Co Chanel.

I do not think I have ever seen Anna look bad. Her long legs, groomed jet-black hair and olive skin, turned men into mush wherever she went.

No one really understood our relationship, least of all my sister Joyce who thought she was nothing but trouble, describing her as "too loose for her liking." However, it was my three years away at Nottingham University that bound us in a way I did not think possible. Being away from home was hard, I kept thinking it would get better with time, but it never did. My experiences at school left me guarded, continuing to build a wall that would keep everyone but only a very select few away. Looking back, I now know that it was a lost opportunity. I wasted the chance to spread my wings and find myself. I knew how hard it had been for my parents to send me there, so in order to make it easier for them, I started various part-time jobs, mainly in bars and restaurants, which left little time to frequent the University bar or many student events. However, what I lost on one hand I gained with the other; my work made me more confident and able to mix with people of all ages, from all walks of life. Regardless of the circumstances, I was careful not to give too much of myself away. I built a reputation for being a recluse; I even heard rumours that some of the girls in my halls thought I was a little stuck up. At the time, I was hurt, scared that history was repeating itself. Maybe if I had tried to mix more, get to know these people, I could have broadened my horizons, found friends, some even for life.

I would look forward to my visits from Joyce and Anna, who would come laden with gifts of mum's home cooked fried chicken and glorious fresh, moist Jamaican rum cake. These tastes of home, accompanied by a cup of tea, would bring me pleasure on long cold nights spent studying, trying to get my head around a particularly complex legal concept.

I noticed immediately how Joyce and Anna's relationship developed, laughing and joking, not noticing how unusual this was. No doubt, spending hours sharing the long drive to Nottingham allowed them the much-needed time to get to know one another. I guess mum was right when she said, *people soon learn to get along when they are thrown together on a sinking ship.* I remember feeling a little jealous of their newfound friendship. Now, years later, we are back to the status quo with Joyce and Anna returning to keeping a healthy distance but always aware of the common denominator between them.

* * *

"I bet you haven't even called your mum."

"Anna, you are determined to make me feel guilty, anyway I've had about a million missed calls from Joyce."

"Well I suggest you give her a call pronto before she sets up surveillance outside your flat."

"I'll call them later, I've got to get on with some work. Listen, I'll speak to you after work."

"You'd better, I'm off today so call me when you get home, we'll have a natter."

"Yes."

"I mean it Pats ..."

"Yes, yes later. I've got to go."

I was about to start on some work, but thought better of it, deciding to call mum on the back of Anna's guilt trip.

"Hi mum." I knew what was coming and was prepared for it.

"Oh so yu remember dat yu 'ave a mother?"

"Sorry mum, I've just been really busy at work."

"And yu tink dat excuses yu selfishness? Patsy, yu 'ave to do better, yu know. Yu feget dat every day me and yer farder is getting older. Patsy Cunningham time is precious ... every day yu have wid yer mother and farder is a blessing; you 'ere what I'm telling you." My mum was brilliant at piling on the guilt, which only sounded more convincing when amplified through her strong Jamaican accent. "Patsy yu working too hard, yu need a break. You tink I don't know that yu work until

God knows what time inna the middle of de night. Hold on I'm going to get yer daddy."

"No mum I don't need to speak to …"

"So you're still alive. You know how many times yer mother try call you. Patsy you must pick up yer phone, you know?"

"Sorry, I was working dad. I promise I'll be round this weekend. Tell mum I'll see her on Sunday."

"Is every ting alright?"

"Yeah dad, everything's fine. Tell mum I love her, and love you too. I'll see ya Sunday and I'm really sorry for not calling."

I just had one more call to make and I knew it would be the hardest. "Hi Sis."

"I am so not talking to you, why don't you ever return my calls? I had this picture in my head that my baby sister had been bludgeoned to death by a jealous lover."

"Joyce, you are always so dramatic."

"Have you called mum?"

"I just spoke to her and dad and before you say anything, I'll be there this weekend, alright?"

"Don't do it for me. They're only the two people that have looked after you since you were born and went without so that you and I could live a decent life."

"I'm going now, I'll see you on the weekend."

"What's wrong, your voice sounds funny?"

"Nothing's wrong, I'm just a bit tired that's all." The biggest disadvantage to having a sister that knows you so well is she can always tell when you are hiding something.

"I'm going to call you later and you better pick up that phone or I promise you I'll be down there, do you hear me? All work and no play, get a life Patsy!"

I guess I was lucky to have a family and friend that cared so much about me, but it was all about self-preservation. Work was my safety blanket. It stopped me from thinking. Mum, Dad, Joyce, even Anna, all they ever did was remind me that I should start living. Why couldn't they accept I was happy with the way things were?

* * *

By lunch, I had gotten through most of my outstanding work, and was extremely pleased with myself. I set my heart on a large baked potato with lashes of butter and cheese. I hated the calories but loved the taste and consoled myself with the fact that I would work it off later on my Wii Dance 3. On my way out, Mr Rawlings summoned me into his office. I cursed under my breath, wondering why managers always call you as you are about to leave.

"Sorry Patsy I know you're on your way to lunch." *Then let me go,* I said, to myself, *of course.* "I just needed to run something by you. I think it would be of great interest to your team."

"What can I do for you Mr Rawlings?" I deliberately do not remove my coat.

"I've had a call from a very successful Legal practice firm," Mr Rawlings shuffled through mounds of papers.

"Ah here it is. Templeton and Rye Legal Practice of barristers have offered to conduct a training session on the recent changes in Environmental Law and procedures and, more importantly, they're offering their services free of charge. Apparently, they were very impressed with your performance at court yesterday." Suddenly I lost my appetite.

"Patsy I am sure you understand that with the financial constraints upon all local authorities, when a barrister's firm as prestigious as this offers a free training session, we would be mad not to snap their fingers off." I wanted to tell Mr Rawlings to let Templeton and Rye know where they could stick their training, but of course thought better of it.

"I agree that this would be good for all concerned so I'll get one of my staff to liaise with Templeton and Rye. Tina can take care of it, this will be good experience for her."

"I hope you don't mind Patsy but they want to move quite quickly and they have specifically asked for you, so I've taken the liberty of checking your diary and have arranged a meeting with you and Mr Templeton for this afternoon."

"What? I'm on my way to lunch Mr Rawlings and have loads of work to get on with, I'm still catching up from yesterday after covering for Melanie." I protested.

"But you've finished the advice on the Hastings Report which, as usual, was excellent. This would be quite a feather in the team's cap if we were to pull it off."

"Frankly I'm surprised Mr Templeton can find the time to see me on such short notice."

"He assured me he had an opening in his diary. Apparently he was trying to contact you yesterday but was unable to get hold of you."

"I was in court all morning and took the Hastings file home to work on."

"You don't have to explain yourself to me Patsy; I know how hard you work."

"Thank you Mr Rawlings." I replied through gritted teeth.

"The appointment is booked for three o'clock. Here are the details." I wanted to stuff those details down his throat but, once again, thought better of it when I remembered I still had a mortgage to pay.

On leaving Mr Rawlings office, I returned to my desk to do my research on Templeton and Rye; fore-warned is forearmed. I intended to walk into the mighty Colosseum and face battle with the legal lions suitably prepared. Adamant, this time, I would not get caught out. It seemed this was my week for being forced into difficult situations. First Melanie, now this; well if bad things come in threes, maybe I should adopt the Iranian approach; crack an egg in the hope of ending it.

When I was finished, I did something I had not done in a long time. I made my way to the Spencer's Arms and ordered a large glass of white wine, probably not advisable on an empty stomach, particularly as wine goes straight to my head. Richard Templeton had done everything he could to manoeuvre me back into his line of fire and, to be honest, I was not sure how to deal with that, so I guzzled down the wine, hoping it would provide me with an answer. Unfortunately, it didn't.

Chapter 7

༁

The wine loosened me up, but I still had knots in my stomach as I sat outside the large office and waited for an audience with Templeton the Great. A feeling had been gnawing away at me since yesterday and I had deliberately immersed myself in various tasks in my attempt to keep it at bay. Oh God, I had been so rude to him! Why was I so rude? If I'd known for one second that I'd be seeing him again, I would have thought twice about using this big mouth of mine to such good effect. My head was swimming, brought on by an adrenalin boost assisted by the sauvignon ... thank the Lord for Tic Tacs.

"Can I get you a tea or coffee?" The friendly face of a mature woman stood over me.

"No thank you." I was too nervous to accept anything, just in case I spilled it everywhere.

"Mr Templeton will be with you in a moment."

"No problem." I hated feeling so insecure in these unfamiliar surroundings. The woman returned to her desk and began working very efficiently whilst I tried to distract myself with pointless magazines on luxury home living. The offices were so posh, nothing like the dreary surroundings of my own grey cluttered office.

"Hello." Richard Templeton glared down on me, a favourite past time of his. He was as pristine as ever in a grey suit, white shirt with a matching grey tie, so accurate you would have thought it had been fixed in place by a spirit level, and there again that hint of cologne, which was subtle but, dare I say it, very sexy. I could feel eyes following me into the office but held my own, greeting each look with a defiant smile.

"Please Miss Cunningham, take a seat."

I heard the door close behind me as Richard made himself comfortable behind a large desk. I guess I should have felt awkward, yet, his office was warm, cosy with its plush carpets, mahogany desk and bookcases. A few pictures sat in pride of place before him; I wanted to examine them but did not have the nerve. Annoyingly, I found myself avoiding his gaze. He had this way of staring at me, which gave me the feeling he was looking straight through to the back of my neck. Richard said nothing for what seemed an age, until I could not stand it any longer.

"So Mr Templeton did you summon me here for the benefit of my health?"

"You're still very direct aren't you Miss Cunningham?"

"Well nothing has changed since the last time you saw me, which was all of yesterday Mr Templeton."

My heart was beating at an unusual pace and I was beginning to regret having that large glass of wine.

"Was it really only yesterday? It seems a lot longer than that." One of the powerful things about being a dark skinned black woman is that you have the perfect camouflage when embarrassment kicks in. All I can say is, thank God for camouflage.

"I can assure you it was only yesterday. Maybe if you utilised your time more effectively perhaps it would not pass so slowly."

Richard's smile broadened. "Why did you refuse to take my call?"

"To be honest Mr Templeton I am a little confused. I thought you asked me here to discuss this training session you wanted to put together." *Stick to the point Patsy, do not waiver, show no fear*. I watched as he loosened the buttons on his jacket and removed it, placing it on the back of his chair and reverting to that familiar stare, as if preparing to cross-examine me.

"Where are you from?"

"How is that even remotely relevant?" I snapped.

"Let's just say I'm curious, humour me."

"Well far be it for me to stand in the way of your curiosity Mr Templeton." I kept saying his name, hoping that it would intimidate him, undermine him in some way, which usually worked with other adversaries. Unfortunately, this tactic did not work with Richard.

"Miss Cunningham, why do I always get the feeling you're telling me off."

"I have no idea what you mean." I knew exactly what he meant but I was hardly going to admit that my childish tantrum was merely a way of protecting myself from how he had made me feel from the first moment I laid eyes on him. That he was the most amazing and sexiest thing I had ever seen. Sitting in front of him was so difficult and avoiding his gaze was becoming almost impossible because there were only two of us in the room. I decided to humour him.

"If you must know, both my parents are Jamaican and I was born here. My dad's a builder and my mum works as a care officer in an old people's home now; before that, she was a machinist and a very good one."

"They must be very proud of you."

"They are and I'm very proud of them ... So Mr Templeton, your turn." I retaliated, and he obliged without hesitation.

"My mother and father live in a small village in Derbyshire. They are both retired." I waited for him to finish because he knew I would not leave it until I heard the rest. "Before retiring my father was an eminent surgeon and my mother was a very stern sister working on a busy hospital ward." That both surprised and pleased me; I considered it a worthy profession.

"And I suppose you're very proud of them too."

"Very. At least that's one thing we have in common. I knew we'd find something." How could he think we had anything in common? We were so different it was laughable, but before I could respond there was a knock on the door.

"Forgive me for intruding on your meeting," A man stuck his head around the door.

"As usual Rupert your timing is impeccable." Richard beckoned the man in, he seemed pleased with the intrusion. "I'd like you to meet Miss Cunningham from Bramfield Council." I started to get up but the distinguishing man beckoned me to remain seated.

"Is this the young lady that you were telling me about?" Rupert may have been asking Richard the question, but his eyes never left mine as he gently took my hand.

"The very same," replied Richard. He sounded strangely proud, as if showing me off, which only added to my embarrassment. It was bad enough having him in the room, now I had to contend with two of them.

"Rupert Rye, pleasure to meet you" Rupert made himself comfortable on a small cream sofa.

"Nice to meet you too." Well I couldn't think of anything else to say! I felt cornered so had to be nice. Anyway, he seemed harmless enough so I decided to play the game.

"I understand you locked horns with our Richard yesterday and left him with a bloody nose," Rupert was studying me intensely.

"Believe me, Mr Rye he got off lightly. He walked away with a caution! The least I could do was sting his client for costs, which I think was a fair and proper outcome." Rupert laughed aloud.

"I cut my teeth in the criminal law courts, spent five years working my way through the Magistrates and Crown Courts, bail applications, and trials dealing with the most unscrupulous reprobates."

It was hard to imagine someone like Rupert Rye in the chaotic world of the criminal law courts. "Did you enjoy it?"

"Every damn minute of it!" Rupert bellowed, clearly excited at being able to reminisce on more exciting times.

This larger than life character, who I took an instant liking to, intrigued me. "Then why did you give it up?"

"No money in it, commercial law is much more lucrative." Rupert whispered.

"Tell me about it!" I was amazed how easy it was to talk to him.

"Richard tells me that he's looking to set up some training for you."

"Free training" I emphasised.

"You really are on the ball Miss Cunningham." Rupert responded.

"Let's just say you need your wits about you when you're dealing with the likes of Mr Templeton, who I dare say, could talk his way out of hell and into heaven, as well as getting the devils employed by Lucifer to pay his taxi fare all the way to those pearly gates." Richard continued to invade me with his silent stare but said nothing. Rupert on the other hand, was engrossed.

"She's got your measure Richard!" Rupert was clearly a successful man, yet, there was no pretence about him. I could understand why he and Richard were partners. I was thinking now would be a good time to build on that rapport, now that I had their attention.

"Right. My guess is that you're offering this freebie in the hopes of somehow getting your foot in the door of the local authority."

"Go on." Richard finally broke his silence.

"Judging by your clientele, you focus on very lucrative company law involving importing and exporting, but you do have a small criminal sect which deals mainly in Environmental breaches. This is but a small part of your business and therefore you are looking to expand in this area. Well I think we could mutually benefit one another in this respect. I know that you are probably lining up some basic training but I'm afraid that's not quite what I had in mind. I am looking to build a very good team and in these lean times, it is all about bringing money in.

"What do you have in mind?" asked Rupert, interest peaked.

"The government have provided the way, and I need you to provide training for my staff and my clients in that area."

"You're thinking of POCA," said Richard intrigued

"Yes. The Proceeds of Crime Act, to be exact. If we go after individual businesses who break the law by let's say building a block of private flats without appropriate planning permission, then charge high rent for those flats to unsuspecting tenants, this Act allows us to claim that money back. The beauty of it is, it hits them where it hurts, in their pockets and as you know these types of businesses have very deep pockets. Yet, the problem I face is this is a very complex area, requiring details of bank accounts, properties, shares you name it. These businesses are very good at hiding their assets, and when we go after them, they will be coming to the table armed with legal heavyweights, and for a local authority strapped for cash, that can be a worrying prospect. Nevertheless, I am of the opinion you have to speculate to accumulate and for that reason, I want you to provide training in this area."

"What's in it for us?" Rupert's business head was firmly in place.

"The head of my legal department, Mr Rawlings, was very interested in me coming here today; he knows the reputation of Templeton and Rye. I have worked with him for a number of years; let's just say he trusts my judgment. I will be happy to discuss the possibility of instructing your firm to act on behalf of the Council, at a reduced rate of course, which will ultimately give you a foot in the door."

"This is pretty risky, what if you don't win, you stand to lose a lot of money." Richard interjected.

"The percentage of nothing Mr Templeton is precisely that ... nothing. In any event you don't strike me as the type of person who factors in the concept of losing." I watch as Richard and Rupert look at each other and mulled over my proposal. I knew they were in the business of making money and what better way of drawing them in?

"I must say Patsy, can I call you Patsy?" asked Rupert and I nodded in agreement "Someone with your brains could make a killing in commercial law."

"The problem with the legal profession, Rupert, is that a number of people tend to judge the book by its cover, which places a lot of us at a disadvantage. I mean let's take your firm for instance; there appears to be a distinct lack of colour." I knew I was overstepping the boundaries, but I could not help myself.

"It's funny you should say that Miss Cunningham, because I have been meaning to do something about that for some time," replied Richard. He stopped me dead in my tracks, as all three of us knew exactly what he meant. There was an uncomfortable silence as I finally allowed my eyes to meet his, terrified at what I now know is about to happen between us.

"Well I'd say that I am now surplus to requirements," Rupert finally said. "Patsy, it has been a pleasure. I'll leave Richard to handle the details, but I know we will see each other again," said Rupert, kissing my hand. In normal circumstances, this action would have appeared out of place, but I found the gesture surprisingly charming, as Rupert was a true gentleman.

"I'll look forward to it Rupert." I said with honesty, suddenly nervous at the thought of being left alone with Richard. As he left the room, Rupert gave a fleeting glance to his partner that should have been a warning signal for me to leave, but I didn't.

"What made you come to court yesterday?" I asked, trying to work out why fate was dealing me this hand.

"Aalie Jordan is a loyal and trusted friend and I would not have entrusted the case to anyone else. He is a very good man, whose only mistake was leaving the running of his business to inept and incompetent people. I was not about to let anyone destroy his livelihood and a criminal conviction would have done that." It showed an unusual loyalty which I did not expect from someone in his position, but my protective shield was going nowhere, and at that moment it was telling me to leave, get out quickly while I was ahead. Richard was not holding back, he was beginning to open up to me and I was not sure I was ready for that.

"Well it's getting late. I'd better be going. I'll e-mail my proposals first thing."

"Have dinner with me" said Richard as I got up to leave.

"You really are unbelievable." I said nervously, gathering up my bag and coat and desperately trying to get to out.

"Is it so wrong to want to get to know you better?"

"I'm overworked and underpaid and that's all you need to know." Richard remained amazingly cool as he sat back in his large chair.

"You're not going anywhere."

"Tell me something. Was all this just a ruse to get me here?"

"Partly."

"Well at least you're honest."

"Patsy I'm a man of my word; we will be providing the free training and in the area you want."

"You'd better" I said, turning my back on him and escaping towards the door. Suddenly, I felt a breath wisp over me like a cool summer breeze, and a heavenly mist of cologne transported me to a mysterious place, where there was no room for fear or inhibition. Should I open the door and walk away, or should I face my fear? I was tired of running. I decided to turn toward my fate as Richard extended his arms around me and prevented me from leaving.

"Stay, Patsy, please." His voice hummed through me, making me feel as if we were the only two people in the world and as he drew closer and our lips met for the first time, they felt warm, soft, silky. The tips of my fingers gently ran through his thick, black hair before finding their way to his sculpted face. His strong arms encased me within them, our mouths opened and we caressed each other with our tongues. He held me so tightly that I could hardly breathe. Through the palpable silence as our lips continued to entwine, I could hear someone making noises of pure ecstasy and realised it was me. I felt his hands between my legs, it felt too good to stop him. There was a rush of blood to my head as I allowed him to lower me to the floor. His lips teased at my neck as he carefully began to open my blouse, one button at a time. This feeling, the depth of it was overwhelming. Every touch awakened dormant sensors in my body taking me to a place I had never been before, a place I had kept hidden because it would leave me open, vulnerable.

"You are so beautiful," Richard said, whispering in my ear.

"Richard … please … I can't breathe …" I remained in a trance as he covered my nipples with his sweet, wet lips, gradually discovering every part of my rich dark brown skin. Captivated by his tenderness, we were engrossed, mesmerized by one another. I knew every explosive emotion that I was feeling was wrong, yet, it felt so right. I revelled in the joy brought on by each touch. I actually stopped thinking and allowed my body, my mind, to drift into an intensity of sensuality, where there were no rules. It didn't matter that we had only met a few hours before, I wanted him and nothing I could do, would change that. So, I let myself become part of the moment, allowed this gorgeous man to encapsulate me, and steer me towards physical ecstasy.

* * *

Richard brushed Patsy's cool, dark, smooth skin, cherishing every second; an adrenalin rush had taken hold of him fuelled by excitement. He could feel his heart beating through his chest as Patsy slowly removed his shirt, he rested his bare skin on her waiting breasts and his body trembled. He guided her towards the zip of his trousers; her hand was warm, she lowered the zip and stroked his penis, which was impatient to be inside her, yet, he held back and basked in the sweetness of their moulded bodies. He gently pulled away Patsy's skirt, revealing her small black panties, which he carefully drew down, leaving her naked beneath him. Richard lifted himself over her; he wanted to look into her eyes so that he did not miss a single expression. The fact that Maggie could have walked in on them only added to the danger, the reckless abandonment was exhilarating and he did not want it to end, but he wanted Patsy, his body ached for her and he could not wait any longer.

Richard's dark blue eyes seeped through me, as if searching for my inner soul, I knew he was ready, yet, "Richard ... wait ... what about ..." It was then that I saw the glimmer of silver wrapping.

"Shhhh ... ready now baby?" It was then I knew I was safe, so I invited him in, I felt a sharp but welcome pain as he thrust inside me; it took all my will not to scream aloud in complete rapture. Richard moaned, I quickly covered his mouth and he sucked at my fingers in a frenzy, penetrating relentlessly as we lost ourselves in the immense pleasure and thrill of the moment. I was engrossed in overwhelming elation where, for the first time, I felt free. Our passion built towards its climax; I threw myself whole-heartedly into it. There were no half measures, no holding back, imploding within each other, bringing a sense of completeness, contentment.

We lay there amongst the discarded clothing and held each other for a long time, disregarding the fact that someone could have burst in on us at any moment. Then, as the bliss faded and reality broke its way through the haze of satiation, I suddenly felt mortified that I could have allowed something like this to happen. I was lying, naked, next to a man that I met less than a day before. Any self-respect that I may have had was disappearing fast. I finally summoned the courage to lift myself up and begin to get dressed. I was covered in shame, not because I hated myself for what I had done, but because I enjoyed it so much.

"Aren't you going to talk to me?" asked Richard, which I suppose was his feeble attempt to try and ascertain where the land lay between us.

I grabbed my disorganised bundle of clothes. "What do you want me to say?"

"That you don't regret what just happened."

"You'd better get dressed before someone comes in." I said, side tracking the issue. Richard rose and began dressing. By the time he was ready I was heading for the door.

"Don't leave it like this Patsy; at least have dinner with me, we can talk."

"About what? This was a mistake, it won't happen again."

"This was what we both wanted from the first moment we met."

"You don't know me Richard, you don't anything about me."

"I know I've never wanted anyone as much as I want you"

"I suppose you're used to getting what you go after, I'm proof of that. Well, for the record, I don't feel good about what's just happened, and if you expect to see me again, don't hold your breath." I rushed out before he could stop me. I don't know how I must have looked, but I just needed to get out as soon as possible. I headed for the lift and detoured into the, fortunately empty, ladies room. I found a cubicle and locked myself in, leaning against the clean white walls and trying my best to regain some composure. It took several minutes for my heart rate to calm down and when it finally did, I slowly made my way out into the plush ladies room with its velvet chairs and designer soaps. I studied myself in the mirror. I had no idea who the person staring back at me was. Things like this simply do not happen to someone like me. I do what is expected, I am a good person and care about right and wrong. My parents brought me up with morals; they have always been proud of me, everything I have achieved has been worth it, just to see the pride in their eyes. How could I face them on Sunday after what I had done? As for Joyce, she knows me better than anyone, it would be hard to keep this from her but the truth is I could never tell her what I have done. She wouldn't understand, not even I do.

I checked my hair and clothing; everything was in place so I left, pressing the buttons of the lift repeatedly in the hope that it would get me out sooner.

Out on the street, people were all around me, but I saw and heard no one. I was dazed, stunned, unaware of where I was going. Therefore, when the hand grabbed me and pulled me into a small side street, pinning me up against the wall I simply let it happen. Richard was breathing heavily, without his jacket and all so crisp familiar tie. He held me, penetrating me with those eyes, he drew me towards him, kissing me tenderly on the lips.

"You can be in denial all you like Patsy Cunningham, but take it from me, this is not the end, it's just the beginning." He kissed me again and then he was gone.

Chapter 8

✿

"OMG, I do not believe you, Patsy Cunningham why are you lying to me?"

I was thankful for the solace of my best friend, even when she questioned my sincerity.

It seemed only yesterday that we sat in this very room in the middle of Anna's small lounge in her top floor flat going through every solicitor firm in the yellow pages, sending my CV to everyone in the hope of landing a prized training contract. As the rejection letters arrived, Anna would make me store them away in a bright yellow folder because that was my favourite colour, pushing me to keep sending quoting *A girl should be two things: who and what she wants.* I kept telling myself I may get a million no's but all I needed was one yes and when I finally got it, we were ecstatic. Buying an expensive bottle of Champagne, shaking it for dear life before we opened it and drenching ourselves, resulting in us only tasting a drop.

Now, once again, I was confiding in my only friend, telling her the gory details. Saying it aloud, I could understand why she was finding it difficult to believe. "So you're telling me you and this Richard ..."

"Templeton ..."

"I need a drink" Anna disappeared into the kitchen and returned with a large bottle of white wine and two glasses. She knelt down next to me on the floor and passed me one of the glasses, which I took, despite having work the following day. Anna filled the glasses to the brim. We both took a large sip. I got up, walked over to the small window and watched some children riding their bikes below, thinking only of Richard.

"Patsy come and sit down."

"I can't, I'm too excited, too scared. If I sit down for too long I'll have to think about how disgusting I've been."

"But what was so wrong about it?"

"Anna!"

"What?"

"Didn't you hear a word I said? Didn't you hear what I just did?"

"All I know is you've just experienced something most of us can only dream about and forgive me for feeling just a tad jealous. Imagine it, while all those people were outside you were in there, on his floor making ..."

"Anna please! I can't bear it, I feel sick. How could I do such a thing? How could I even think about doing such a thing?"

"You did it because you fancied the pants off him literally ... this calls for chocolate."

Once again Anna jumped up, ran into the kitchen and returned with a large box of Milk Chocolates. The box was already opened as Anna placed it on the floor, carefully picked one and shoved the box in my direction. I refused and, against my better judgement, drank some more wine. I still felt his arms around me, his breath on my neck, his strong arms holding me down, and wondered if he was thinking about me too. Anna helped herself to another chocolate and guzzled the wine.

"The question now is how do you intend to seal the deal?

"Sorry you've lost me."

"Chances are there's a queue a mile long for a catch like this Richard, but after your recent exploits I'd say you've propelled yourself to the front of that queue."

"You make him sound like a prize bull."

"That's exactly what he is and the sooner you get to grips with that fact, the better."

"It could never work," I told her.

"Why?"

"Because I'm here on earth and he's way up in the stratosphere, that's why!"

"What's so different about him? He's a man isn't he? Opposites attract, you know."

"Yeah he's a man alright, gorgeous, handsome, successful … and then there's me; I'm just a working class lawyer trying to make ends meet."

"Patsy Cunningham don't you dare sell yourself short."

"I'm not, I'm just being practical about the differences between us, that's all."

"So you're just going to walk away from the chance of a lifetime?" Anna asked.

"You don't understand! He's like no one I've ever met. When I'm around him, I lose all sense of control and I hate that."

"And what's so wrong with losing control once in a while? The trouble with you, Patsy, is the law has made you too methodical, you can't do anything without thinking it through."

"You know what I'm like Anna, I put everything I have into my job because it's all I know, all I'm good at and now … Oh God!" I was close to tears, in tatters. Anna led me to the sofa and placed her arms around me.

"Alright, calm down. I understand why you are finding it hard to take all this in, no pun intended … but I just need to know one thing before you walk away from this experience of a lifetime. How did it make you feel, letting yourself go like that?" I wanted to answer but felt so guilty saying the words aloud that I just took another drink. "Come on Pats, it's just you and me, tell me how this Richard Templeton made you feel. Jesus you've made a career out of stringing meaningless words together, surely this can't be that difficult."

"I can't, anything I say is just going to sound really corny."

"Patsy love is corny, it's … marshmallows and candy floss and all that crap, that's what makes it so wonderful you silly cow. Now drink up and tell me!"

I finished the glass, Anna promptly re-filled it and I took another large sip, which helped me to find the words. "Alive…he made me feel alive…"

"Go on."

"It's as if there were these senses lying dormant in my body and in that short time Richard found every single one of them. Now they're tingling inside me, waiting for their next fix. He's set off a chain reaction all over me that I just can't stop."

"Wow, what are you going to do?"

"The only thing I can do, stay as far away from him as possible."

"Okie dokie, let me know how you get on with that one."

Chapter 9

❦

Wednesday

I crashed as soon as my head hit the pillow, which was a good thing because I really needed a good night's sleep. I woke up nursing a hangover, with Michael Buble's *I'm feeling good* ringing in my head after Anna made me listen to it at least a hundred times. *There's a time for wine and chocolate, but sometimes you need 'the Buble'"* she kept saying, doing her best to indoctrinate me into her make-believe world of hearts and flowers.

I decided to reject her questionable words of wisdom, throwing myself into researching recent case law on the Proceeds of Crime in preparation for the training. After my confident presentation yesterday, it was important that I was fully versed on the subject. I was determined to remain focused, accepting that the events of yesterday afternoon were nothing but a blip on an otherwise untarnished record. In life there has to be to room for error and the unconscionably sordid act a few hours before was mine. It was a lapse of judgement; could have happened to anyone caught off guard by an expert in manipulation, wrapped in the immaculate package that was Richard Templeton.

God it suddenly dawned on me, what if the training was no longer on the table, now that Richard had what he wanted? What is stopping him from withdrawing his offer? How would I explain that to Rawlings? I breathed a sigh of relief on finding an e-mail from Maggie Anderson, PA to Richard Templeton, which confirmed that training was arranged with a list of convenient dates. Despite still being shell shocked by the unexpected events of yesterday, I was pleased that Richard remained a man of his word. I had no idea how I could face him again, and thought about booking leave on the day of the training, but that would have been too awkward. I decided to cross that bridge when I came to it.

As I eagerly researched various pages, making my notes along the way and frantically printing relevant material and highlighting important areas, Anna's words continued to resonate. Yes, I am methodical; I have to be because a lawyer requires an analytical mind, but has it made me a colder person? Maybe. I am someone who is frightened to open up and let go. What's so wrong with having a strong hold on your emotions? If you ask me, it keeps you sane. Losing control can land you in all kinds of trouble. Look what happened when I gave in to impulse yesterday! Someone could have walked in on us! I would have been completely humiliated and probably out of a job. I needed to stick to what I knew and not veer from that; it's safe, comfortable.

I had arranged a meeting with a client that morning at their offices, so went straight there. It was a difficult meeting with the client presenting me with a number of demands, to which, of course I had to agree, but knew I would have to work twice as hard. Everybody always expected so much, I just wished they could get their heads around the fact that there was only one of me. I was pleased when it was over.

I arrived back at the office just after eleven and, of course, was greeted by the customary Post-It note left on my computer by Mr Rawlings requiring my undivided attention. As expected, I had to provide him with a blow-by-blow report of the meeting with Templeton and Rye. Like most avid networkers, he was more interested in Richard and Rupert than the actual training itself. He had the cheek to raise concerns at the thought of me daring to suggest the Proceeds of Crime, complaining that as the training was free, it was not our place to make demands. I made it clear, however, that it would be a fruitless exercise to waste anyone's time on an ineffective session. As I continued to work my magic, he began to come round to the idea, particularly when I explained the possible financial advantages. I could see the dollar signs in his eyes, aware that he would lay claim to the idea and present it as his own, but that didn't concern me. I wondered what kind of spin he would have put on my extracurricular activities.

On leaving Rawlings' office, my team immediately bombarded me with questions on urgent cases, none of which could wait. I dealt with each one in a practical fashion, astonished at how well I had managed my morning. While the events of yesterday afternoon still lingered in my mind, I kept my focus on work, determined not to let it hinder my busy day. When I logged onto my phone, I found three messages waiting for me:

MESSAGE ONE: *Good morning Patsy, Denise here. Good news; Mr Jordan came in and signed the caution and paid all our costs in full. Great news about the training I can't wait. Do you think Mr Templeton will be running it? Speak to you later.*

MESSAGE TWO: *Hi Pats its Anne. Hope you're ok. I am nursing the mother of all hangovers. I'm gagging to talk, I didn't sleep a wink, call me.*

MESSAGE THREE: *Good morning Miss Cunningham, this is Lacey's ringing to confirm your 3.30 appointment for this afternoon, If there are any problems, please do not hesitate to contact us on...*

I must be going mad because I do not remember booking an appointment … and who are Lacey's? They must have the wrong number, but they mentioned me by name. I wondered if this had anything to do with Joyce. She was always doing stuff like this; arranging things without asking me first and just assuming that I would do it. Without thinking, I called my sister. Her response was both perplexing and typically Joyce: "Lacey's? Do you really think I've got the time or money to do that? If I did, I'd book it for myself! They've obviously got some promotion going on, but how did you get on their mailing list? They are really exclusive. Just give them a ring … or better still, say nothing and just turn up. They may be giving away some freebies and, if they are, remember I'm your sister."

There was no way that I was going to give Joyce the satisfaction of admitting that I had no clue who Lacey's were, so I googled them. I definitely knew a mistake had been made on discovering that Lacey's was an exclusive boutique situated on Cavell Square which specialised in Lingerie and high-class evening wear. I was even more surprised to learn that private fittings were arranged by appointment only. I was not sure what to do but felt that if a mistake had been made, it would be best to clear it up. For all I knew they could have muddled me up with another Patsy Cunningham and how did I know they would not try to stick me with the bill? It could be a fraudster who got hold of my details.

I needed to get to the bottom of this, so took my mobile into the library and closed the door.

"Hello, my name is Patsy Cunningham. You left a message on my voicemail about an appointment for 3.30 today?"

"On yes, one moment Miss Cunningham, I'll put you through to private fittings." After a brief interlude of classical music, another voice answered "Private Fittings."

"Hello um … my name is Patsy Cunningham…"

"Oh yes Miss Cunningham, your fitting is arranged for 3.30 this afternoon, is there a problem?"

"Well actually I don't seem to recall making the appointment and I was wondering if you could …"

"Not at all Miss Cunningham, I'll just check the details … Oh yes the booking was made this morning in the name of Mr Templeton. Will you be keeping the appointment Miss Cunningham? … Miss Cunningham…?"

I have come to the conclusion that there are two different types of women in this world: those that take and think nothing of it, and those who never take and are proud of it. Where do I fit in? Well I'd like to consider myself as being too proud to say yes but not stupid enough to say no.

"…Miss Cunningham…?"

"Yes … I'll be keeping the appointment."

"We'll look forward to seeing you at 3.30 … and Miss Cunningham, we pride ourselves on our discretion."

Chapter 10

※

I describe myself as a workaholic. Making my way into the office on a Saturday morning to catch up on work was not unusual, and I did this despite the fact that I was not being paid and it would not even contribute towards additional time off. My colleagues, would regularly lambast me for this. It would have made more sense if I were working for myself, but putting so much energy into a faceless entity was just not practical, because the more you did, the more they expected of you. That did not stop me from doing it.

Therefore, you'll understand when I tell you that skiving off work that afternoon with the lame excuse that I had to tie up formalities surrounding a caution that had already been signed and sealed was very much an aberration.

I tried calling Richard but was informed by the very efficient Miss Anderson that he was, coincidentally, tied up in conferences for most of the afternoon. What kind of man does something like this and then does not even have the decency to tell you about it? Apparently, precisely this type of man. I had never been to a private fitting of any kind. Even when my sister got married, we were all crammed into one room at our Aunt's house tripping over each other whilst being measured. I had a feeling that this was going to be a very different experience. The one redeeming feature was that Richard was clearly not going to be there. I rushed home, leaving a trail of clothes throughout the flat as I threw myself into the shower. Even though my mother would be very ashamed of my antics right now, there was no way I was going to put, what she would call, *'shame in her eyes.'* I decided to wear my dark blue high Court dress, secured from a sale at TK Max, which was classy and elegant and worked well with my best underwear from Marks and Sparks that would ensure I concealed any knicker line, a thing I found very unbecoming. I threw all the contents of my jewellery box onto the bed and frantically searched until I found my ivory receding pearls and matching earrings, determined to walk into Lacey's with the small measure of decorum I had left. I applied my make-up with meticulous precision and thanked the Lord for my GHD's which tonged my short Halle Berry cut effortlessly. I hated wearing high heels during the day but decided to weather the storm in my higher than usual ASOS shoes, which were a steal at seventy-five pounds in the sales and were surprisingly comfortable. I calculated that I had a wearing time of just a few hours before they would start to pinch, but how long could it take to try on a few items of clothing? If there was ever a time that I needed Anna's advice this would be it. She would have no trouble decking me out to perfection, but I could not risk telling her, because nothing would stop her from coming with me and I wanted to do this on my own. Besides I still was not sure about whether I was actually going to go through with it and at least if I were alone I could walk away without seeing the disappointment in her eyes. Nevertheless, I think she would be proud of my bold step. As for Joyce; she was never afraid to speak her mind where I or anyone else was concerned, therefore, I decided to lock her in a box and store any opinions she might have in the back of my mind.

I remember the last time I went to Cavell Square; it was on my way to a training course in the City. I could count on one hand the number of times I had been there; well I never make a habit of frequenting areas where there are no prices in the shop windows. I am of the opinion if you can't see a price, you can't afford it. Suddenly, I came to the realisation that I actually had no money, well not the kind of money that I'd need for somewhere like Lacey's. I had been jumping to the conclusion that Richard would be paying. They never even mentioned money when I called. Do I mention it or do they? But then again, if he set this whole thing up, why wouldn't he pay? Alternatively, if I was an independent woman, why would I let him pay? What would he think of me allowing him to pay! *Shut up Patsy Cunningham and get ready.*

Lacey's was everything I expected. Situated on the corner of Cavell Square with a beautifully sculptured silhouette in the shop window, I was about to take the mammoth step through the large revolving doors when my mobile went off.

"Hello."

"Patsy, it's yu mother, I cannot talk for long because I'm on my mobile." My mum always spoke very loudly and very slowly when she was using her mobile, something we had all resigned ourselves to. She would never spend more than a few minutes talking, convinced that it was costing her hundreds of pounds per minute.

"Hi mum." I walked away from Lacey's, fearing that somehow she had a bird's eye view of my specific location at the time.

"I'm in Tesco's and they are selling one large bottle of Ribena for half price. You want me to get you a bottle? I know you love ya Ribena." My mum was the queen of bargain hunting. If she saw a bargain she'd grab it, whether she needed it or not, storing it away like a squirrel in the large cupboard under the stairs.

"Ok ... thanks ... Get me a bottle mum, that would be good. Thanks." I said tripping up on my words.

"Alright yu can pick it up on Sunday when yu come."

"Ok mum. Listen I've got to go. I'm on my way to a meeting. Love you." I quickly ended the call, not wanting to hear my mum's voice any longer as it felt like a warning to stop all this foolishness and get my arse back to work. The simple fact was that mum was blissfully unaware of where I was and what I was doing. Besides it's like Anna said, I'm not a child, I'm a grown woman with a mind of my own to use as I wish and I'd definitely come too far to let a guilt ridden discounted bottle of Ribena stand in my way.

As I entered, it struck me how few people were there. Lacey's, with its tasteful off-pink walls and elaborate prints, was a delight and refreshingly relaxing.

"Good afternoon, can I help you?" said a very slim young woman who had no right to be that pretty, wearing a pair of heels that I would have needed a ladder to climb into.

"Hello, I'm Patsy Cunningham. I have an appointment for 3:30 today." *Why are you telling her it is today? You would not be here if it were booked for tomorrow! Calm down Patsy.*

"Please come this way." I followed the young woman through a long passageway leading to a lift. "If you could take the lift to the third floor, someone will be waiting for you." I stepped into the lift and smiled, too nervous to say anything in response. I pressed for the button for the third floor and waited impatiently.

When I reached my destination, the doors opened and an older, refined woman greeted me.

"Miss Cunningham?"

"Yes."

"Good afternoon and welcome to Lacey's. My name is Helen Fuller, I am the manager here, so if you have any problems please do not hesitate to let me or one of my staff know. If you would follow me to reception."

"Thank you." I was not used to this five star treatment and to be honest found it all a little daunting, but did my best to keep it together. At the reception, Miss Fuller asked me to sign in.

"Can I take your coat Madam?" another young woman said, who was waiting by the reception.

"Yes ... thank you." The lady put my coat on a gold velvet hanger, and placed it on a large wooden rail behind the spacious reception. "I know this may sound a little strange, but can I clarify the position in relation to payment?" I asked Miss Fuller, not looking up from the register.

"Oh that's all been taken care of Miss Cunningham."

"Right" I was thankful that my mind had been put at rest. I could not help wondering what she must think of me. Miss Fuller then summoned over another young lady.

"Janice can you take Miss Cunningham to fitting room number seven please?"

"Yes of course," replied Janice, an equally attractive young woman who I followed down another long corridor. I was shocked to find that the fitting room was only a little smaller than my bedroom. There were large mirrors on two sides and a small table contained an ipod on a docking station, which was playing classical music. These people think of everything! There was also a cushioned chair situated next to a rail containing a selection of white lingerie and two beautiful evening dresses.

"These are the items that have been selected Madam" Janice made her way to the rail, where she removed two pieces of clothing.

"The sizes range from ten to twelve and as you can see the purchaser has impeccable taste."

"Why are they all white?" I asked not thinking for a second that this may sound slightly ungrateful.

"Because that is what the purchaser requested Madam, and may I say he has chosen particularly well."

"It's just that I associate lingerie with black, normally."

"Most people do Madam, but believe me, this is the right choice for you. Now before you commence your fitting can I offer you a complimentary glass of Champagne?"

Oh My God! "Yes that would be lovely." I didn't have the nerve to say I didn't really like Champagne and that I always needed to mix it with orange juice to make a Bucks Fizz, but somehow I did not think that a request of that nature would go down very well in Lacey's. Janice disappeared and returned a few moments later carrying a glass of Champagne on a tray, which she rested on the small table. The Champagne was accompanied by a small selection of chocolates enclosed in a gold box.

"Please accept our complimentary chocolates and if you require any assistance please do not hesitate to ring this bell. Enjoy your fitting Madam." Janice left the room and closed the door behind her. I immediately went over to the table and stuffed the box of chocolates in my bag. I knew I could not eat them now! What if I got some on the clothes? And I had no intention of leaving them.

I could just about take it all in; Here I was in Lacey's when only a day before I didn't even know they existed. Boy, how the other half lives! I went over to the rail, slowly surveying the various items of clothing, not knowing where to start. They were all so beautiful. Janice was right; Richard had impeccable taste. I had never seen anything like it. It reminded me of one of my favourite films, *Rebecca,* where Mrs Danvers holds up an exquisite lace nightgown for Joan Fontaine, asking her, "Have you ever seen anything so delicate?"

A gorgeous, white lace Kimono Robe with a matching thong beckoned to me. It felt soft in my hands as I held it up in astonishment. In Mrs Danvers' words, "you could see right through it." I replaced it and moved onto a White Mesh, Corset-Style Bustier set with a matching G String. I wondered how I was going to get into it. The hooks were so delicate, but luckily fitted from the front. However, it looked a little small and there was only a ten. What if it didn't fit? I was beginning to panic and needed to calm down; I took a small sip of Champagne. It tasted nice! This was definitely the good stuff, so I took another sip, and felt a warm glow as it ran through me. I decided to keep looking as I wanted to relish every moment and the longer this experience lasted the better.

I found a Corset in matte silk taffeta; God knows how much this cost. It was incredible, with padded cups and a double laced skirted hem, which would do wonders for my hourglass figure. It came with matching suspenders, thongs and white stockings. I had savoured the moment long enough, this I had to try. I quickly removed my dress and underwear, hanging it carefully on the rail. The corset felt different to anything I had tried before, literally sculpting my figure. I guess when things are designed to precision this is how they are supposed to fit. The Private Fitting room was so spacious it was like being in my own bedroom, minus the Champagne and discarded clothes of course. I was determined not to look in the mirror until I had the entire outfit on because, although it felt right, it would have broken my heart if it did not look how I imagined and I wanted it to be perfect. There was a small clasp at the back of the corset, which secured a bow in place, but for the life of me I could not reach it, after a number of failed attempts, I decided to ring for assistance and was relieved to hear the door open.

"I'm sorry." I said not bothering to look around. "I seem to be having a little trouble with this clasp" I bent down and point to the offending area. "I know there's a knack to this." I felt a hand fastening the clasp into place.

"Thank you." I said.

"My pleasure," Richard replied. I froze on the spot.

"You look incredible." I could feel Richard's welcome breath on my neck as he gently brushed his fingers down the sides of my naked arms. I shivered. "Do you know how beautiful this looks against your gorgeous skin?" He moved closer to me and slowly stroked my neck with the tips of his fingers.

"I was under the impression this was supposed to be a private fitting." I whispered, shivering a little.

"You can't get more private than this, Patsy." Richard caressed the contours of my body. "Your skin is so smooth" he continued, pressing me into him, stroking my thighs as his fingers found their way under the lace thong, Our bodies moulded together whilst he rubbed my crevice. I shuddered, tensed as Richard softly pushed his fingers inside me. I moaned and rested my head into his broad shoulders, receptive to him as he delved deeper and deeper, taking short sharp pockets of breath the further he indulged.

"Look Patsy, look at how exquisite you are." Richard told me and, completely obedient, I slowly looked up and see myself in the mirror for the first time. This could not be me. It was as if I were outside myself, watching a woman I did not recognise, a woman who had allowed herself to be manipulated, intruded upon, but against all her better judgment, she welcomed his invasion. She reached out to it in a way that she could never have imagined. I continued to watch myself, outside this body, and waited for this beautiful, voluptuous, sexy woman with her striking dark brown skin against the white taffeta to object, demand he stop. However, she knew, I knew, those words would never be uttered, because that woman was me. Richard pressed hard against me; his warm touch burrowed further and further, soaking my insides, making his intrusion all the more pleasurable. He pressed against me and I reached behind me to grab the back of his neck. I begged for more. Our eyes met in the mirror and I was greeted by that familiar stare behind an immaculate grey suit with crisp panels slightly revealing a white handkerchief neatly tucked away in the lapel, with that hint of Gautier. Richard slowly withdrew, releasing me. He turned me towards him and I welcomed his kiss. He smiled as he stroked my hair, examined my face, shoulders, arms, legs in tender motion, as if seeing me for the first time. I savoured every moment, utterly submissive to his will, with each touch breaking down that wall of granite, one brick at a time.

"You are so lovely." As Richard said the words, I no longer felt uneasy because I was beginning to believe him; not out of vanity or ego, but because I wanted to. His seduction continued as he ran the taffeta through his fingers. "Tell me what you're thinking Patsy."

"I am not thinking, because I'm too scared of what will happen if I do." I was content and submerged into every touch.

"Then I suggest we seize the moment, for however long that may be." Richard whispered.

"And how long do you think that will be exactly?" I asked, knowing I had ventured into forbidden territory.

Richard began to unclip the delicate hooks on the front of my corset and his silence put any hope I had of longevity between us into perspective. Nonetheless, I respected that at least he did not lie to me. He made no promises. The corset gave way, revealing my hard nipples. Richard cupped my breasts in his hands and I closed my eyes, relished the moistness of his tongue as he expertly worked his way towards my inner sanctum. He kneeled, fully clothed, drawing down my thong. I was completely bare before him as he kneaded my buttocks and pulled me towards his expectant tongue and burrowed his way in. I used my fingers to part the way, allowing him full access. My insides throbbed as

I pressed myself harder against him and tugged at his thick black hair whilst he continued teasing me. I groaned in ecstasy, savouring the moment, wanting, no, needing more, but Richard suddenly pulled away, making his way over to the rail where he removed the Lace Kimono.

"Come here." He said, I followed his instructions, taking my naked body towards him with no inhibitions. I stood unquestioning, allowing him to wrap the Kimono around me gently tying it from the front. He then reached into his inside pocket, and pulled out the small coloured box containing our protection, which he gently placed in the pocket of the Kimono. "Something I intend to fully utilise ... later." Richard made me shudder with excitement at the realisation of what he had planned for me.

"Richard I want you to know I've never been like this with anyone. You have found a side of me I never knew existed. The truth is I don't know who I am anymore." Richard pulled me towards him and kissed me gently.

"You are a vibrant, amazing woman who should not feel guilty for being treated once in a while."

"But this is hardly in the same league as a bunch of flowers or a box of chocs, babes."

That was the first time I called him that and it showed just how relaxed I was around him. I flicked through the rail and sighed as I took one last look at the two white dresses that I did not dare try on; because

I had no intention of keeping them. The first was a sweetheart neck line, full-length white dress with silver trimming. I could feel the tight bodice and could only dream about how outstanding it would look. The second was a white and black strapless mini dress, which looked like the stuff dreams were made of.

"Richard I can't accept these."

"Why not?"

"You've spent enough and besides it would be a waste of money. Where would I wear them? They are not exactly run-of-the-mill, are they?"

Richard looked carefully at the dresses, removing them from the rail. "Well if that's your only problem it is easily solved. You can wear this when I take you out to dinner tonight, and this" said Richard, holding up the long evening dress "you can wear when I whisk you away to a secret location on Friday."

Chapter 11

꙯

"Richard there is no way I'm walking through that restaurant in this dress without my coat." Richard ignored me as he removed my coat and handed it to a man who took it quickly.

Richard pulled me towards him and whispered "Cast your mind back to what we were doing this afternoon. Hold that thought, because if you don't behave I'll never do it again."

"Why Mr Templeton resorting to blackmail, frankly I'm disappointed that someone of your calibre would stoop so low."

"Shut up and walk." Richard said as he discreetly slapped my bottom and escorted me through the crowded restaurant. All heads turned at the sight of an attractive black woman in a posh restaurant wearing a strapless dress which clung to her like glue. Richard was amazingly cool. Nothing fazed him as he moved his hand to the small of my back, leaving no room for doubt that we were together. I loved his confidence and his ability to take control. Granted this worried me at first, yet now, it seemed natural that I allowed him to manoeuvre me in the direction that he wanted to go. Anything else would be to swim against the tide, it was easier to relax, close my eyes and let the stream take me where it would. God, this was the first dress that I had ever owned with a hemline above the knee. Anna would be livid that all her efforts had been in vain. All it took was a man I had known for less than forty-eight hours to unleash the Ms Hyde in me; there was no need for mixed potions or scientific calculations. My transformation was brought about by a very different kind of chemistry.

I could not work out if the looks we received were ones of disapproval or envy. Richard nodded, acknowledging the odd stuffy face here and there who smiled politely. A waiter skilfully pulled out my chair to seat me. I thanked him politely.

"Just don't order snails, or frog legs." I said softly as Richard patiently mulled over the French menu.

"Are you ready to order Sir?" The waiter stood efficiently at our table.

"Thank you yes, the lady will have a have a Poulet Frites and I think I have the Pot au feu."

"Thank you Sir." Richard waited for the waiter to leave before telling me.

"That's chicken and fries for you and beef stew and mixed vegetables for me. Not a snail or frog's leg in sight."

We talked non-stop during the meal. I made an effort to stay away from the wine, as I was conscious that I had consumed more alcohol in the last three days than I had in the past month, however, I was unsuccessful in my endeavours with the waiter continually re-filling my glass, which I felt obliged to empty. I had never been a lover of red wine, but the food tasted so good and the wine seemed to compliment it, so it seemed a shame to waste it. We talked about everything from music to films, our likes and dislikes, we even discussed work, having a somewhat heated discussion about who worked harder, a solicitor or barrister. Yet, we were careful to avoid anything about our life and the individuals in it. We deliberately stayed away from that subject and it had been such a wonderful day that I was not going to do anything to spoil it. At the end of the meal, I asked Richard if we could go into the piano lounge and without hesitation, he agreed. The bar was quiet with just a few people holding conversations, not paying much attention to the hard working piano player who must have been there for hours as it was past eleven. I insisted that we sit near him and Richard ordered the drinks.

"Will you be alright while I nip to the little boy's room?" Richard asked.

"I'll be fine." I replied. A small group of women entered the bar and they must have had a fair amount to drink because they were quite boisterous. The piano player continued, oblivious to the disruption.

"Do you want me to tell them to keep it down?"
I asked the piano player.

"No I'm used to it" he replied.

"Am I allowed to ask your name?"

"Harry."

"Harry! You don't look like a Harry." I said,
surprised.

"What does a Harry look like?" he asked as he
continued to play.

"Not like you." Harry smiled. "Am I disturbing you?"

"No it's nice to have a beautiful woman to talk to."

"Why thank you Harry."

"You're welcome."

"Patsy, that's my name, Patsy."

"Nice to meet you, Patsy"

"Nice to meet you too, Harry." I was actually quite
tipsy with the champagne accompanied by the two
or three glasses of wine at dinner. I do not know if it
was that noticeable but I think it might have been.
As Richard returned to the bar, I saw how the women
observed his every move. *Read it and weep ladies,*
I said, to myself, *of course.*

"Richard, meet Harry and Harry, this is Richard."

"Pleased to meet you, Harry" Richard said, giving a
small nod of approval.

"Likewise" replied Harry, continuing to play.

"I've come to the conclusion that Harry does not
look like a Harry." I told Richard.

"Have you now" Richard smiled broadly.

"Yes." I tried to stop that muscle in my mouth controlling my tongue from flapping but the drink had worked its way so far into my system that it had taken over my vocal chords. "I used to sing you know, I know people must say that to you all the time Harry, but I really did. When I was at University I worked in a Jazz bar and had to sing sometimes, some people thought I was pretty good." I had never confessed that to anyone but Anna before, not even Joyce knew. Alcohol is a dangerous and wonderful thing.

"Patsy Cunningham you never cease to amaze me," Richard stroked the back of my neck attentively.

"You ain't seen anything yet. Harry do you know *The Nearness of You?*"

"One of my favourites."

"Will you play it for me?"

"It would be my pleasure,"

"Thank you Harry." I leaned over the piano and without warning grabbed the mic. "How about you and I stir this place up a bit?" Harry had already started the introduction to my request. I turned to Richard and began to sing.

It's not the pale moon that excites me
That thrills and delights me, oh no
It's just the nearness of you

It not your sweet conversation
That brings this sensation, oh no
It's just the nearness of you

When you're in my arms and I feel you so close to me
All my wildest dreams come true

I need no soft lights to enchant me
If you'll only grant me the right
To hold you ever so tight
And to feel in the night the nearness of you

Richard absorbed every word, I did not realise anyone else was listening until I heard the applause. Richard grabbed me off my stool, lifting me off the floor as he kissed me, which was also greeted by applause.

"That was incredible!" he said genuinely moved by my performance.

"Told you I could sing," I replied with a self-satisfied feeling that came uncomfortably close to arrogance but at that moment, I was so happy I did not care.

Richard gave Harry a big tip, accompanied by an even bigger hug from me, and I waved goodbye, a little worse for wear as Richard led me away, praying that we could come back one day. I even had the most forbidden dream of all; maybe, just maybe if things went my way, I could dare to dream that he might even play at our wedding. No sooner had the thought popped in than I dismissed it, accepting that a wish as extravagant as that could not possibly come true. Fairy-tales are make-believe, and that's precisely where they should stay. Outside the restaurant, I was still shaking from my unexpected performance and Richard wrapped his jacket around me and told me to hold on while he hailed a black cab. It did not take him long to find one and he helped me in with the bags.

"Where to mate?" said the cabbie.

"The Ritz" Richard replied.

Chapter 12

౪

What woman is content with her body? There is always something about herself that she would like to change. For some of us, it is the dreaded bingo wings, a too soft tummy or those jiggly thighs. However, I can truthfully say for the first time in my life, there was nothing I wanted to change about me; I felt perfect. A more empowered woman would ridicule me, argue that it was wrong to allow my feelings about myself to be determined by a man's treatment and if I were the same Patsy Cunningham of two days ago, I probably would have agreed with her. The fact was, I was no longer the same. Was I a better person? I very much doubted it, but was I more enriched? I would have to say yes.

I always considered myself a snob in the bedroom because there were things I would do and things I just would not. It is not that I was a selfish lover, it's just that I believe in equality and unfortunately, when it comes to sex women are at a disadvantage. To begin with, we don't have as many orgasms as men and half the orgasms we do have, we fake, which we only do to make the man believe we have enjoyed the experience. Anna says she does it because she just gets bloody tired, or when she likes a guy and does not want to disappoint him. She told me nothing boosted a man's ego more than when he thinks he has achieved the dizzy heights of making a woman reach a climax in ecstasy. If nothing else, she found it extended the life of a relationship by at least an extra couple of months. You see the thing is, women think and feel all the time, even when they're making love.

However, once in a while, you find the rarest of men, one who doesn't just think about himself but also about the woman he is with. I realise that they are the ones who get it right, because when they take the time to give you pleasure you don't have to fake it.

Listening to Gladys Knights *The Look of Love* while Richard held me in his arms in a suite in the luxurious Ritz Hotel in nothing but my new Lace Kimono was confirmation that there was heaven on earth. Our bodies were made for each other and what scared me was after being with him, I did not think I could ever be with anyone else. As he raised me up and pinned me against the wall, gently suckling on my breasts, I understood the meaning of true pleasure. I held his erect penis firmly in my hands, he was so hard I was a little apprehensive about how painful it might be, but with Richard, I looked forward to the pain. He carried me over to the bed lowering me slowly, but this time

I wanted to be in control. Straddling him I pulled off the lace belt of my Kimono and covered his eyes with it.

"You've given me the best day of my life, now I'm going to give you the best night of yours." I slowly crouched over him licked and kissed his naked chest as I worked my way down to that part of him that I wanted inside me so badly, because if I gave him what he wanted he would do the same for me. He was so hard! I stroked him before I gently nipped at the head, Richard flinched. I steadied him with my other hand pressed onto his chest. "Don't move," I murmured.

My tongue slipped up and down and he twitched in response. I steadied him and continued to massage his immense tool. I moved slowly up and down, all the time securing him with one hand. Richard moaned aloud and my insides pulsated at the excitement I created in him. I wanted to take him whole into my mouth but I made him wait, rubbed at the penis, now hard like stone, up and down before I wrapped my tongue around it and worked my way from top to bottom. Richard groaned as I held him down, I was in control now and I loved it! I felt the immense power over him at that moment, which was more tantalising than anything I have could ever have anticipated; I opened my mouth and slowly closed it, drawing him in gradually through my lips, working my way up and down until I reached the middle. I licked the rim of the head of his penis taking him further, sucking gently as I edged my way down and finally swallowed him whole. I felt him tense. He was ready to succumb to me but I could not let that happen. I wanted him inside me, so I slowly pulled my mouth away, kissing his tip and eased the ribbed covering over him, before guiding him inside me. I was so wet he slipped in easily and I began to ride, pushing him further and further into me I rocked up and down. Richard grabbed my buttocks, squeezing them, slapping at my naked behind. I loved it! It hurt yet felt so good that I begged for more. I could feel my whole body exploding from within and I knew my time was coming. Richard suddenly pulled himself up, threw me on my back yanking my legs over his neck and rammed into me. He was so hard as he reached deep inside that I screamed for more. He grabbed the cover from his eyes and impatiently enveloped my lips with his, our tongues were lost in each other and, as he sustained the onslaught, I felt my soaked vagina bursting and knew that I was close, very close.

"Baby don't stop I'm going to ..." I said as Richard continued slamming harder and harder, I closed my eyes and could think about nothing but the immeasurable pleasure this man brought to me. Richard began to clench his teeth and I knew he was also close. I wrapped my legs tight around him digging my nails deep into his arched back. We both rocked in this perpetual motion until neither of us could hold off any longer, simultaneously igniting tidal waves inside one another.

Chapter 13

✿

Thursday

Two men observed as Richard and Patsy left the Ritz, arm in arm. They watched as Richard wrapped his arms around Patsy and kissed her gently before placing her in a waiting taxi. One of the men snapped busily away on his fast frame camera, capturing every moment as Richard waited until Patsy's was out of sight, then disappeared into a black cab which waited behind. One of the men reached for his phone.

"They've just left, what would you like us to do? … Right … follow the girl."

Chapter 14

I felt seventeen again, sneaking in past my curfew. Why did I feel so guilty? I'm a grown woman who has done nothing wrong; a text came through as I entered the flat and I impatiently read it, hoping it was from Richard. It was!

"Hi you, did you get home alright?"

"Yes how about you?" I text back

"It's nice to see you're in one piece." I screamed at the top of my lungs as Joyce confronted me at the front door.

"Joyce! You nearly gave me a heart attack."

"Join the club. Where the hell have you been?" I could not believe the cheek of my sister! I pushed past her and made my way into the bedroom, Joyce followed me. This was all I needed! I had to get showered and ready for work.

"How did you get in?"

"I used my spare key."

"Er, I think you'll find it's my spare key, which you're only supposed to use in emergencies. Joyce you can't

just let yourself into my flat as and when you like."
I heard another text come through but had no choice
but to read it later.

"For your information, I classify my baby sister
doing a disappearing act as an emergency. I tried getting
hold of you all afternoon and through most of the night.
I even came down here after midnight only to find an
empty flat and no sign of my sister. I called Anna, who
was acting very cagey but wouldn't tell me anything.
Look at the bags under my eyes! I haven't had a wink of
sleep." The onslaught continued while I pulled off my
coat and started to undress.

"Where did you get that dress?" Shit, I knew I should
have put the TK Max back on but I loved my new dress
so much I wanted to wear it home. How was I supposed
to know Joyce would be waiting for me?

"I bought it, people do that you know."

"Where from? You never buy dresses above the knee
and it looks pretty exclusive to me. Where'd you get it
Patsy?" Joyce was suspicious.

"A shop alright. Joyce please, I've got to get ready
for work." I prayed she would relent, but my sister was
as determined as ever to get the answers she was after.

"What are you doing with a Lacey's bag? I thought
there was something funny when you asked me about it
yesterday."

"What is it with all the questions this morning?"
I rushed into the bathroom, turned on the shower and

was not surprised when Joyce followed me in, carrying the bag.

"Where did you get this Pats?" Joyce held the bag up in front of me.

"Do you mind?" I attempted to grab the bag but Joyce had a firm hold on it. "Joyce that's mine and I want it back." Completely ignoring me, my sister began to delve inside the bag and pulled out the Lace Kimono.

"Now what do we have here?" Joyce waved the Kimono at me. I grabbed it from her but she had already pulled out the taffeta corset and bustier. She carefully examined the lingerie. "These are originals. Do you know how much stuff like this costs?" I watched as Joyce pulled out my gorgeous white dress and at that point, I decided that I had to try to bluff it out. I calmly took the dress from her and headed for my bedroom, aware of her presence throughout. I opened my wardrobe and hung the dress up very carefully. I then proceeded to open my chest of drawers folded my lingerie away and closed the drawer slowly, coming to the conclusion that now would be a good time to call a truce.

"Listen I'm sorry I didn't ring. It was really selfish of me and I promise it will never happen again." I could see from the look on Joyce's face that she was unconvinced.

"Are you going to tell me where you got that stuff and don't even think about lying to me Patsy

Cunningham because until yesterday you hadn't even heard of Lacey's."

"How do you know that?"

"Because I know you, you'd never buy anything like this for starters. It's not you and anyway, you couldn't afford it; this dress alone must have cost over a thousand pounds and you don't have that kind of money to throw away on clothes. Please Patsy you're scaring me." I loved my sister but sometimes it was difficult having such an intense relationship. For some inexplicable reason, Joyce blamed herself for the scars of my past, angry that she had not been there to protect me when I needed her most. She had never understood that she was not responsible for my torment. She watched over me like a lioness over her cubs. When she married, I thought things would change but they never did. I was her baby sister and she was never going to let me forget it. I suddenly realised how selfish I had been. When I moved out of my parents' home and into a flat of my own, we made a promise that we would call each other every night; a deal I had clearly broken. I went over to Joyce and gave her a hug and she reluctantly did the same.

"I'm sorry, I really am. I promise it will never happen again and if you must know ... I've kind of met someone."

"How can you kind of meet someone? Either you meet them or you don't."

"Alright I've met someone."

"And who is this someone?"

"He's just a guy."

"Apparently a very rich guy. It's not like you to take anything from anyone. You must really like him."

"Well it's early days." Oh God why did I say that?

"Just how long have you known this person?" Me and my big mouth!

"A while," I said, trying to dig myself out of this hole before I was too far in.

"Early days doesn't equate to a while Patsy. How long have you've known this 'guy,' and remember I can always tell when you're lying."

"I don't want to talk about this anymore. I'm going to have my shower."

"Oh no you don't," Joyce said yanking my arm.

"Ouch you're hurting me."

"How long Patsy. I said how long?"

"A few days alright, just a few days. Three to be exact." I whispered in shame deliberately avoiding eye contact. Joyce let go of my arm sitting on the end of my bed and I hated the disappointment in her eyes. I sat next to her.

"It's not as bad as it sounds, well maybe it is but from the minute we met there was this spark between us and I tried to fight it, I really did but he's got this way about him and it's just …"

"He's not a drug dealer is he?"

"What ... No ... what do you take me for?"

"Pats you are my baby sister, I know sometimes you think I'm hard on you but that's only because you mean the world to me. I wasn't there when you needed me before, but I'm here now; and I will never let you down. I want nothing more than for you to be happy, you believe that don't you."

"Yeah ... I believe you; and I love too Sis, but you're always going on at me to get a life. Well now I've got one."

"This isn't exactly what I had in mind, you've known this man for all of five minutes and you're letting him buy you all this stuff, and spending nights away."

"You've got no right to lecture me. I'm not a child, I'm a grown woman and you can't tell me what to do." I did not know where this defiance was coming from but I felt the need to defend myself.

"You know what, you're right." said Joyce heading for the front door "Who am I to tell you what to do? You wanna take stuff from this guy, fine. You wanna sleep with him, fine. Just don't come running to me when it all goes wrong."

I run after Joyce and stopped her at the front door.

"Joyce you're not going to say anything to mum and dad are you?"

"What so that mum can have an asthma attack and dad can come round and kill him and then you? No, I won't say anything, but that's not for your benefit it's for theirs. You need to check yourself Patsy because none of this is going to end well. You're heading for a fall and right now. I don't even recognise you."

As Joyce slammed the door behind her, I felt bad that I had clearly hurt her. Rather than dwell on the moment, I went to my bag and checked my phone where another text was waiting. "Call you tonight, can't wait to see you tomorrow."

Chapter 15

Richard Templeton had an insatiable need to succeed. Not just for himself but also for his father and mother, John and Martha Templeton. His parents had groomed him to believe nothing was impossible, telling him from an early age that he must find something he is good at and work hard at it, but always with humility and integrity. It was not easy growing up in the shadow of John Templeton, an eminent surgeon, but Richard's brilliant mind and confidence allowed him to carve out his own niche. Clearly, there was an element of disappointment when he decided not to follow in his father's footsteps and enter the medical profession, choosing to set his sights on the lower bar of law, but the shallow man within him wanted a more lucrative career and one which came without such dire consequences when you lose.

He wondered what his parents would have made of his recent exploits, which were difficult enough for him to understand. What was going on in that complex mind of his? Where were those values that had been conditioned and instilled within him? Unlike everything else in his life, his adventure with Patsy had not been planned. He did not suddenly wake up one morning and think; today I am going to become a liar and a cheat. Until now, he had stayed on that trusted road with no turns and clear signs, but for the first time he was in unfamiliar territory, confused.

Work had always been his controlling factor, allowed him to excel and make an extremely comfortable living. It seemed an age ago that he grappled his way through the hustle and bustle of his first legal firm, with other young, hungry barristers. It was a battlefield, where the words 'integrity' and 'humility' were irrelevant, as everything centred on outdoing and discrediting your opposition. However, Richard was excellent at the waiting game, steadily working his way through smaller less lucrative cases, building a reliable clientele who would make recommendations to others. He steered away from criminal matters, knowing that economically, this was a dead-end road. He was happy with his regular work and safe clientele, building his knowledge in the less interesting area of civil damages claims. Regardless of the lack of excitement and regular comments from his peers that he did not have what it took to net a big case; he continued working hard and steadily.

At first, the Jordan case was like any other. There were no raised eyebrows when the small brief landed on young Richard Templeton's desk after a previous client had recommended him. Richard met Aalie Jordan for the first time at his home, as he was unable to travel to Richard's offices because of the serious injuries sustained from an accident at work. Richard's instructing Turkish speaking solicitors acted as translators for Mr Jordan who, despite being in great pain, insisted on meeting Richard away from his sick bed. Richard remembered how the proud man refused any help, scolding his family whilst they fussed around him. Richard tried not to show any pity as Mr Jordan stumbled towards the large armchair, having lost his right leg in the devastating accident. The room had a deadly silence whilst his two teenage girls remained at the table saying nothing and as his wife placed the Turkish Apple Tea on the small table by Richard; he could smell the spices as they filled the room. Although, Mr Jordan's words were being relayed through a third person, Richard felt an affinity to this man whose story uncovered the most extreme callousness one seldom comes across. As he scribbled the facts in his notebook, he wondered how it could be possible for anyone to work twelve-hour shifts, with only a one half hour break, no protective equipment at such low pay. Yet Mr Jordan smiled and laughed as he spoke about his life, loves and need to provide for his family. It was equally hard for Richard to fathom how Aalie's employers could try to wash their hands of the incident by offering such a measly sum in compensation. He eventually realised that, to them, the Aalie Jordans of the world were no more than a mere irritation.

There were to be many visits between Aalie and Richard, many court appearances and many senior barristers watching as the case unfolded. Pressures came from all sides to allow a more senior barrister to conduct the advocacy due to take place in the High Court, but Aalie was adamant that he wished Richard to hold the reins, stating he trusted him and knew that, win or lose, Richard had faith, which was all he needed. Standing to his feet before His Honour Judge Roland, with his faithful client sitting behind him, Richard was scared and unsure of himself, which placed him at a disadvantage against his more seasoned opponent. As Richard looked around the large room and opened his case, he found his lips were dry and he had knots in his stomach. It took him a while to find his stride, but he was under an obligation to do the best for his client and after a gruelling two days of examining, cross-examining, labouring on issues of the law and closing arguments, Richard waited patiently for the decision. Aalie and his new found friend and mentor, Rupert Rye, provided comfort and words of encouragement to Richard; with Aalie telling him that it was in Allah's hands now and he must have faith.

In reaching his judgement, His Honour Judge Roland was scathing, not leaving any room for doubt that Aalie Jordan's employers, had acted unfairly and unreasonably to Richard's client. The judge awarded Aalie four hundred and fifty thousand pounds in damages. As Richard listened to the judgement, he could scarcely take it in. It seemed that nothing he had done until that moment mattered, with the case placing him firmly on the map, resulting in him receiving instructions from a plethora of solicitors. Richard was tireless in his defence of his newly found clients and built up an outstanding reputation, taking him from strength to strength. It was not surprising that he won accolades throughout the legal profession, including securing barrister of the year, two years running. When Rupert decided to build his own legal partnership it never entered Richard's mind not to go with him; where they worked hard and built up one of the most successful and lucrative legal practices in the country, with clients all over the World.

As for Aalie Jordan, blessed with a shrewd business mind he used his compensation to open a very successful Turkish Restaurant in the city centre. As the Restaurant flourished, he opened new premises in the much sought after area of Castle Row. It was kismet that the same man that had boosted his career and reputation would be the one to bring him and Patsy together seven years later in Mabley Magistrates Court.

He did not stop to think how Patsy would feel if she found out about his deception but recognised that she was not completely naïve and had some inkling that something was not right. He had always fantasised about being with a black woman, with pure dark cocoa skin, but had never been brave enough to approach one. The few he had met whilst at University never really mixed with the mainstream. They were career driven and rarely seen in the University bars, which would have been the only place that would have given him the Dutch courage he needed.

Yet with age came experience and Richard was more confident now than he had ever been and Patsy, well Patsy was special. It was difficult for him to get to grips with the fact that he could feel so much for someone he hardly knew. She fascinated him, bending to his will, as and when he demanded. He did not think this was love; an overwhelming physical attraction, an insurmountable chemistry had taken hold of him, causing loss of control, all reason. She had become an addiction. The more he had, the more he wanted.

He used to look on whilst his less scrupulous colleagues would go from one deceit to another, wondering when they had reached the point in which they decided to discard their vows of faithfulness. Until now he shunned them, believing he was better than that, worth more, viewing them as dishonest men living discontented lives, proud of his squeaky clean, unblemished image. Yet, Richard Templeton had now joined their ranks, and was a fully-fledged member. He did not condone their behaviour any more than his own, but realised that maybe he had been a little too quick in passing judgement. Feelings have a way of taking you to places you do not want to be, and it is not always that easy to make the right choices in life. After all, he was only human and everyone makes mistakes.

He pulled off the note pinned to the front door of his penthouse flat, *Richard where are you? Call me. Charlotte,* and read the countless text messages left on his phone, deliberately switched off until that morning. It was never his intention to hurt anyone but he was aware that no one would believe him when the truth came out. Until then he was prepared to take his chances, seeing Patsy when and how he could, praying that it would not take him too long to work her out of his system.

Chapter 16

Thursday

"There's no way you can prepare this for court, the instructions are incomplete, where's the land registry documents and the original contracts?"

"I've asked but they keep telling me they can't find them" Mike replied.

"Then send for further instructions, without them we're going nowhere."

I did not think it was possible to have so much work it was difficult to know where to begin, and my disappearing act of yesterday only added to the chaos. Melanie was back on Monday, but had two cases with deadlines for the end of the week. Spoon-feeding Mike, who lacked the balls to make a decision without me, made things no easier. However, being Mr Rawlings' blue-eyed boy meant that he got away with doing the bare minimum, whilst I worked myself into the ground to make sure I met every deadline, even when that meant regularly working up to hundred hours a week. It had always been more difficult for women in the law, and I suppose any other career for that matter.

"I want you to ring the client now, explain the problem, apologise for the delay and then back it up with an e-mail and copy me in." I watched as Mike walked away to make the awkward call and used my will power not to call him back and deal with it myself, which would have been the normal thing for me to do, but I had enough on my plate. My sister's slur on my previously exemplary character still stuck in mind and I hated the fact that for the first time, her pride in me had been replaced with shame. I wished I could introduce her to Richard, get her to see what I see. But what did I see? I hardly knew the man. I had been swept off my feet and onto my back in a day. Joyce was right and after her condemnation I should have done what any self-respecting independent woman would do, pack up all his gifts neatly in a box, return them to him, adamantly refuse to ever see him again and walk away with my head held high. However, for reasons beyond my understanding, I did not intend to get off this roller coaster, and why should I when I was having so much fun? Anyway, I knew I was on borrowed time; the fact that Richard had told me nothing about the people in his life made it clear that he didn't want me to know and I wanted to put any revelations off for as long as possible.

"Ready Pats?" I turned to find Denise behind me, who I had completely forgotten was meeting me for lunch today to go over the final arrangements for the training session due to take place the following week.

"Hi Denise."

"Well don't sound so enthusiastic. Shall I go out and come in again?" Denise planted herself in Melanie's empty chair.

"I'm sorry I've got loads of work going on."

"You've always got loads of work. What you need, Patsy Cunningham is a holiday to take you away from all this." said Denise as she swirled around.

"I wish." God it would be wonderful to be whisked away to a desert Island somewhere; maybe that was Richard's next surprise. I can only live in hope.

"Come on, get your stuff together, we're out of here." Denise was not one to stand on ceremony and before I knew it, she pulled my chair out and grabbed my bag. I could see Mr Rawlings looking at me from his open office door and this was all the encouragement needed to get me up and out.

Denise was a welcome distraction and it was actually nice to take a proper lunch for once. For me, lunchtime consisted of hastily stuffing down a sandwich while struggling to work and take calls at the same time. I knew Denise would have preferred a liquid lunch, but I was determined to stay well clear of that so persuaded her to go to Mario's, the Italian cafe, which did the best cheese and ham omelettes I have ever tasted. Denise worked on the other side of the borough surrounded by an industrial estate, so it was a treat for her to meet me, as my offices were just off the busy high street with all the shops, so of course, before eating, various detours were made. First, into the large shoe shop, followed by HM, Primark and M & S. Denise scolded me for checking my watch as it was clear she was going to make the most of her get of a jail free card. It took nearly an hour for us to get to Mario's and after settling ourselves down and ordering, I noticed Denise eyeing a man seated a few tables in front.

"I swear that guy has been following us, he's been in every shop we've been in and he's here now." whispered Denise.

"It's probably just a coincidence." I said, not bothering to look over.

"One shop is a coincidence but all three and then here?" I discreetly looked over at the man behind, but his back was towards me. The well-dressed man was reading a newspaper and not paying any attention to either of us. Thankfully, the food arrived and Denise's interest in her omelette was sufficient to act as a diversion and as the man got up and left, I was able to convince her that this was simply a case of an overactive imagination.

"I am so excited about next week." Denise sliced her omelette into four squares.

"Den, it's only a training session."

"Err excuse me, a free training session being laid on by one of the most reputable legal firms in the country."

"How do you know so much about them?" I asked, as Denise poured a generous helping of tomato sauce over her omelette.

"I googled 'em and Patsy, that sort of partnership do not offer things like this often. This is a real feather in my cap! My boss is all over me like a rash."

"I'm very pleased for you."

"You could at least try and sound a little more enthusiastic." Denise, had no clue just how enthusiastic I was, but there was no way I could confide in her and tell her the truth about the last few days. As well as being unprofessional, it would have been stupid.

"I am taking this seriously, I really am but it's just that it's a week away and I've got other things on my mind. They'll be sending reading material in the next day or two, so if your team have any issues they should think of them in advance of the session." I noticed that Denise was miles away.

"Denise, are you listening?"

"What about Richard Templeton? Will he be doing the training?" said Denise with a lost look on her face.

"I don't know, they haven't said."

"Well ask! I've told all the girls about him and they can't wait to see him."

"Sorry Den, I've got no say in who they send, so don't get your hopes up."

"Too late, I haven't been able to think about anything else." *Welcome to my world* I say to myself.

"Patsy the man is sex on legs. You know he went to Private School, and then attended UCL, that is the University College London and left with a first class honours degree in Law."

"How do you know so much about him?" I asked, fretting for a moment that Denise and Richard may have had their own dangerous liaison.

"I googled him, it's all there Patsy; his career, relationship, the works." I did not want to hear anymore, but Denise was like a runaway train.

"Personally I think that Charlotte Hemmings is just a flash in the pan; he could do much better." I wanted to leave but my curiosity had me fixed to the chair as I hung on every word. "I mean so what if she ticks the boxes, has more money than she knows what to do with, is relatively attractive, well actually men would say she's pretty hot with a body to die for, but she's not got the ring, so that makes him fair game."

I cannot imagine what Denise must have thought of me after my hurried exit. I made some lame excuse or other, but the fact is the food had stuck in my throat and I felt sick. It was as if my insides were being kicked in, which was only made worse because poor Denise had no idea she was doing it. Each sentence cut like a knife and it was all I could do not to scream at her and beg her to stop. Charlotte Hemmings. Who the fuck was Charlotte Hemmings?

* * *

It is funny how your priorities change. Less than two hours before all I wanted was to bury my head in piles of work. Now my only objective was to find out as much as I could about Charlotte Hemmings and I could not believe how easy it was. How people allowed their personal lives to be splattered across a computer screen was beyond me. Charlotte Alexandra Hemmings, daughter of successful property developers Randolph and Alexandra Hemmings, attended the Bardolph private boarding school for girls until the age of eighteen, and then attended St Andrews University where she studied Literature. I suppose I wanted her to look like she'd been dragged through a hedge backwards, but of course she was perfectly formed and groomed with flawless skin, long blond hair and blue eyes and was only ever pictured in the latest designer labels. Every line I read about her threw me into confusion. I could not understand why Richard was with me. What did he want? He already had it all; it made no sense. One celebrity page described her as an "IT" girl; there were pictures of her everywhere, going to all the nicest places. There wasn't much about her and Richard, one blog described him as her 'latest flame.' What did that even mean?

Clearly, I was a novelty. Why would he take such risks? Lacey's, the restaurant, the Ritz; maybe that was all part of the excitement. Why am I assuming I'm the first person he's ever done this with? He's probably had a string of women and I am only one of many. Well at least I found out now before I got in too deep. It had all been too good to be true anyway.

I am not making excuses for him, but I had known he was hiding something and I deliberately closed my eyes to it because I didn't want the bubble to burst. A few days ago, I was uncomplicated Patsy Cunningham; no problems, no stress other than work. My life was simple and that was a good thing. It was normal and more importantly, safe. I liked being safe. I liked being practical; it takes away any confusion and room for doubt. Now, in vast contrast, I am a wreck of emotions, not sure what I am doing and why I'm doing it. I have let people down and indulged in pleasures with a man I hardly knew in ways that I would never have considered before. When he touches me I could not begin to describe the feeling; it was as if every sense in my body was awake, losing all of control, completely letting go. It is only when it happens to you that you realise how little we do that. We mull along, getting on with our lives, whether we are happy or not, resigned to remain in this "safe mode" whilst we stagnate.

I hated myself for thinking this but the fact was that I only cared about how I felt when I was with him, Charlotte Hemmings or no Charlotte Hemmings. Besides, if she was so good for him, why was he with me? I've always done the right thing, played by the rules, even though I'm sassy and have a lot to say for myself that doesn't make me a bad person. It just means I am a strong woman with a mind of my own. I wish I'd been born with a silver spoon shoved down my throat, but I was not. I dare say she is everything he dreams of, but right now he is dreaming about me and I intend to take full advantage of that.

I've have had to fight for everything, so why should I make it easy for her? So what if she was there first? Life's a bitch and then you die. I'm sick of being good old reliable Patsy. I've had a taste of something else and I love it! Richard Templeton is a gorgeous, sensual man and I want a piece of that. Sure, I'm on borrowed time, but all that matters is I make the most of every single moment I have with him. After seeing her, reading about her life, it's clear that Richard could never love me. Be in lust maybe, but love, no. To him I'm a precious jewel contained within inadequate packaging, not good enough to unwrap and parade in front of family and friends. It hurts that he is using me, yet I only have myself to blame. Why should a man respect a woman who has made it so easy for him? Anyway, it is too late to turn the clock back, so where do I stand, what do

I do? If I confront him, I will lose him and frankly, I am not prepared to take that chance. I am a lawyer with an analytical mind, trained to analyse every situation objectively and based on my conclusions, I have come to the realisation that all I have succeeded in doing is to talk myself into becoming the 'other woman'.

I know that nothing in life comes free, and it is only a matter of time before I will have to pay the price for my decision. Yet, I had given up all hope of experiencing such gut wrenching happiness. Like Cinderella, I am waiting for the clock to strike twelve, where, along with my golden coach, I will transform back into an unwelcome reality of a grey, dull existence. All I can hope is that the magic will linger long after the dream is over since it will have to last a lifetime. Let's face it, Richard Templeton will be a hard act to follow.

Chapter 17

Richard waited patiently in Charlotte's favourite restaurant, mentally preparing himself to begin the uphill struggle of making amends for his absence of the past few days. He was geared up for a long wait, bearing in mind he had kept her waiting, something he knew she was not used to. Like him, Charlotte was used to getting her own way, so the fact that she had agreed to meet him so easily worried him slightly. He ordered a bottle of 1989 white Rieussec. As he sipped the cold crisp wine, his mind wondered back to Patsy singing to him the night before. He had always hated the idea of Karaoke, trying it only once at University when he was very drunk, which resulted in him making a complete fool of himself. He had resolved never to indulge again. However, Patsy's voice blew him away, and even though he was aware she was a little worse for wear, it meant more to him than he cared to admit at the time. His body trembled as he recalled the events that took place in fitting room number seven. The memories of Patsy's body writhing in ecstasy as his fingers were submerged within her flooded his mind. Reminiscing on the sweet taste of her nectar, of her oh so warm innards, he began to throb. He flashed back to the manipulations of the night before where her expert tongue coiled itself around his penis like a Python.

"Penny for them." said Charlotte.

"Charlotte" Richard, taken by surprise greeted Charlotte with a kiss on both cheeks before taking over the waiter's role of settling her down in the chair before him.

"Well are you going to tell me where you have been for the past three days or would you like me to hazard a guess?" Charlotte launched straight in for the attack.

"One of my biggest clients flew in unexpectedly and I had no choice but to drop everything."

"But you could have called Richard."

"I know and I'm sorry, but he was only here for a few days and is a very demanding client as well as our most lucrative one." Richard could not believe how easily the lies rolled off his tongue.

"I've been making excuses all week and frankly am tired of having to justify your constant absences Richard. You know how important this weekend is to me and you have made no effort to get involved."

"I was under the impression it was Isabella's birthday, not mine."

"Don't be flippant Richard. Isabella's a dear friend and the Mansion Party is the highlight of the year;

everyone will be there how do think it will make me look if you don't even bother to make an appearance? Everyone has noticed that you are always the last to arrive at parties and the first to leave." Richard wondered why it always had to be about other people.

"Don't be silly, of course I'll be there."

"Well that's something," Charlotte picked up the menu to peruse its contents, "I think I'll have the Caesar Salad" she said not bothering to look up and clearly pleased that the status quo had now been re-established. She was skilled at saying just enough to keep Richard on the hook, making him work for her forgiveness.

Yet, Richard knew Charlotte well enough to understand that it was all about appearances and it would not have been fitting for her to attend Isabella's party unaccompanied. Besides, she travelled with an elite sect and it did no harm to be around them from time to time, even if they were not his friends.

"Yes, the Caesar looks good. I'm famished spent most of the day shopping with mother. Did you know daddy has decided to gate-crash the party? He really is too much. God knows what he's up to; he was really disappointed when you cancelled on us this weekend."

Charlotte had no idea as she whittled away how Richard was studying her. The contours of her perfect neckline gave her an almost ornamental, statuesque figurine appearance. He found himself thinking how she would fit perfectly behind a glass case, only taken out and admired by an avid collector, not daring to handle her without crisp white gloves. Her picture-perfect body did precisely what she commanded of it. There was not a hair out of place as it rested comfortably on her delicate shoulders. It was a forgone conclusion that she was right for him; a textbook wife on paper. They made a beautiful couple; everyone said so. When they walked into a room, every man envied him and every woman envied her. Yet, Charlotte was like any other woman, using her sexuality to get what she wanted. She dressed tastefully, but always with the suggestion of seduction. She even made love in a sensual but methodical fashion, always participating yet never fully engaging, only doing what was expected of her. Her passion was measured, controlled, making him cautious, wary of trying anything too risqué. Charlotte would never dare venture to the regions of pleasure he had experienced the night before and it would not be seemly to suggest such a thing.

Yet, it was only a matter of time before she would manoeuvre him into popping the question; he had resigned himself to it, like an impending ritual that he must face. Even his parents, who had never pushed him and always allowed him to be true to himself, nudged him towards that final step of marital bliss with the woman who had wasted no time in ensconcing herself into their lives with her excellent breeding and charming disposition.

However, now, Richard was faced with an unforeseen, unexpected twist sweeping into his life in the guise of Patsy Cunningham. Patsy was so different from anyone he had known, with a background that was in complete contrast to the exquisitely dressed porcelain doll seated at the table across from him. Where Charlotte was cool, composed, Patsy was an all-consuming, fiery and feisty original, burning into his every thought, burrowing her way into the heart of his integrity and morality.

"Richard ... Richard, you haven't heard a word I've said."

"Sorry," Richard responded with a blank expression, trying to hide the fact that he was totally lost.

"I said, we will all be travelling down on Friday afternoon so you'll need to pick me up around three, that way we can get some real drinking in," Charlotte went on, unperturbed by Richard's lack of interest.

"That won't be possible I'm afraid," Richard snapped his brain quickly back into gear.

"Why on earth not?" Charlotte returned to an uneasy mood.

"Because I still have a few loose ends to tie up with my client."

"Well can't someone else do it?"

"No Charlotte, this is something I have to take care of myself. I will meet you at the Mansion on Saturday. You can travel up with Isabella. I'll make it up to you I promise."

"Well you'd better because frankly Richard I'm getting a little fed up of this whole thing. I know your work is important to you, but why it has to consume every waking hour I will never know." Once again, Richard had stopped listening; it was as if fate was dealing him an unfortunate hand, throwing reminders of Patsy in every direction. He looked on as the attractive older mixed couple entered the room, the woman smiled gracefully as she was seated at the table directly opposite. Her light brown skin was youthful in appearance and Richard watched as her attentive partner held her hand from across the table. Richard never thought about what it meant to be in a mixed relationship and he had no intention of taking Patsy to the next level as his life was set on a path that he didn't believe could change, but it never occurred to him how at ease he was in Patsy's company until now. Conversations with Patsy were limitless; they wrapped themselves around heated discussions on the law, life, hopes and fears. In her company, he laughed, no, he really laughed and she laughed with him. Nonetheless, he was aware of the elephant in the room, which they both steered clear of, involving any discussion of a future together. He chose to ignore her question in dressing room number seven and she had said no more on the subject, for which he was thankful. Their lives could not be more different but she had opened herself up to him even though he knew it was going against everything she understood and he found himself missing her.

"Well, well if it's not the elusive Charlotte Hemmings."

"Harvey!" Charlotte jumped to her feet in excitement, which Harvey greeted with a kiss on both cheeks.

"Charlotte my darling you look amazing." Richard slowly rose and both men shook hands rather awkwardly.

"Hello Harvey." Richard returned to his seat almost immediately.

"What are you doing here?" Charlotte enquired.

"I'm having dinner with an associate of mine. Why don't you join us? The prospect of a beautiful woman at our table would do us all the world of good." Harvey pointed to the table where a man of Arabian appearance was seated.

"Actually Harvey, thank you for the offer but Charlotte and I have a few matters to discuss, so unfortunately we will have to decline."

"Of course dear fellow, I don't blame you for wanting to keep her to yourself." Richard remained seated and did not respond. "Anyway I take it you'll both be at Isabella's shindig."

"Yes we'll both be there," replied Charlotte looking over at Richard who reluctantly nodded in response, not relishing the thought of spending an evening in Harvey's company, a man who spent his life making an excellent job of doing nothing, prepared to fritter away the wealth he had inherited rather than earned.

"Well in that case I'll see you there." Harvey said as he gently held Charlotte's hand and kissed it before leaving.

"Richard that really was incredibly rude of you; Harvey is a good friend of mine, the least you could do is meet his friend."

"He was not a friend, he was an associate."

"What difference does that make?"

"A lot in my book." Richard watched Harvey return to his table and enter into conversation with the man.

"I don't see what harm it could do." Charlotte insisted, intrigued by the man sitting at Harvey's table.

"Charlotte you are welcome to join them if you wish, but just don't expect me to join you."

"Richard you really are the most rotten spoilsport at times. I'm at least going to have one drink with them," said Charlotte defiantly, leaving Richard at the table as she made her way over to Harvey. Richard calmly called the waiter over.

"I would like to order now please."

Chapter 18

Harvey had failed to make headway after assuring his companion that he maintained some influence over Richard. It did not bode well that he could not persuade him to join them. His one redeeming feature was his friendship with Charlotte, proven by her defiance of Richard, which helped to alleviate some of the pressure but not all. His associates were not known for their patience. Harvey waited nervously in Arif's study, hating what he had become.

Maybe if he had gone to Richard from the start, Richard could have helped him find a way out, but now it was too late, "Embezzlement is a dirty business ..." were Arif's words, as he stepped in to cover all traces of Harvey making his way through thousands of pounds of his father's company's money. What people failed to understand was, once you have money, you cannot live without it. Poor people had no idea how lucky they were. He remembered how simple it was, no one noticed the odd thousand here and there which slowly became tens of thousands and, as he had come from money, no one questioned his lavish lifestyle. It was expected. The more he stole the deeper he sank; but gambling was his Achilles Heel, leaving him with debts spiralling out of control.

The more he gambled, the more he lost, making him careless to satisfy his frenzied need. When questions were asked, Arif knew exactly what to do, stepping in handing him a way out that no one in their right mind would have refused. The alternative was unthinkable. Arif's actions were flawless; as well as replacing the missing money, he made sure anyone who became suspicious of Harvey's actions were silenced, and Harvey was too much of a coward to question how this was done. However, Arif's help came at a price and from that day on, Harvey was required to drop everything at a moment's notice when the call from Arif came.

"Harvey, sorry to keep you waiting," said Arif, entering the large study with two of his men, his greying hair and plump stomach showing a failure to stay away from the finer things in life. He was covered in expensive jewellery, worn with an uncultured pride.

"Not at all," Harvey replied nervously.

Arif settled himself behind a large desk, resting back in a luxurious sofa, churning a glass of brandy savouring it before taking a sip. The door opened and a thin, tall man joined them.

"Ah Hussein, do come in." Hussein approached Arif but said nothing.

"Well?" Arif asked.

Hussein turned to Harvey, eyeing him suspiciously.

"Harvey, would you mind waiting in the other room?" asked Arif.

"Of course," Harvey replied, relieved. Hussein made him feel uneasy and he had no wish to become privy to potentially dangerous information. Hussein waited until Harvey closed the door behind him.

"Is everything in place?" asked Arif.

"It's all arranged, the merchandise will be shipped by ocean freight in four days. I'll be responsible for transportation."

"My man Cassell will accompany you to the Port."

"I work alone."

"It's my shipment, so I make the rules Hussein." Hussein reluctantly nodded in agreement.

"I need those transit certificates," said Hussein, pouring himself a drink from the decanter.

"You'll have them." Hussein made himself comfortable in an armchair immediately opposite Arif, nursing his Brandy.

"Don't take me for a fool Arif," Hussein was aware of the menacing presence of Arif's men who had not taken their eyes off him.

"I'm sure I don't know what you mean."

"It doesn't matter how many people we have on the inside, those documents have to be watertight." Hussein went on.

"I assure you, everything's on schedule."

"Then where are they?"

"Patience" Arif turned to his right hand man, Cassell who instantly left the room, only to return seconds later with Jonathan Southern; the same man who was so desperate to see Richard just a few days before. Hussein looked on as the fragile man entered the room, with Arif's men on either side of him.

"We found him packing and he had these with him." Cassell placed a passport, air-ticket and mobile phone on the table.

"There are a number of calls to and from the same number." Cassell went on.

Arif merely glanced at the phone, then scrutinised the documents before discarding them on the table.

"Planning a trip Jonathan? And you didn't tell me! I must say I am very hurt. Cat got your tongue ... nothing to say?"

Hussein remained silent, waiting to see how things would play out.

"My dear Jonathan, we can make this as hard or as easy as you like, but I think I should warn you, my men can be a little over zealous so it would be in your best interests to talk. Where are my papers?"

"Where's my son Arif?" Jonathan was defiant before finally breaking his silence, as he tried to shake himself free from the men that restrained him.

"I'm sure I have no idea what you are talking about."

"No one's seen him for weeks, what have you done to him?"

"Jonathan my heart goes out to you; I can't begin to imagine how hard it must be to experience the loss of a child; to have no clue of what has happened to them. Maybe you should contact missing persons. I'm sure they could dig him up from somewhere." A sharp pain hit Jonathan, stabbing him in the chest, because he finally knew Roger was dead.

"You promised you would let me talk to him Arif, sort things out!"

"For the last time, I have no clue about your precious son's whereabouts, but wherever he is, whatever rock he's crawled under, I strongly advise him to stay there. Roger was careless. He cost me time and money. Now for the last time, where are those papers?"

Jonathan Southern had spent the last two years of his life planning and plotting his way towards financial freedom. He had come so close to that life of obscurity, where he could put all his indiscretions behind him. Once an honest man, happy with his life, his only crime was over indulgence of a son who lost his mother at an early age and never quite understood what it meant to care about anything. Roger had always been headstrong, wild, demanding. To him money was a doorway into a life he dreamed of and he would do anything to get it, hurt anyone. Jonathan had lost track of the countless times he had come to the rescue of his callous son, who always promised to change but never quite managed it. He continued to hurl himself further and further into a pit of bad choices and even worse company.

Arif was only too pleased to allow Roger the leeway he needed, lending him thousands to support his lavish lifestyle, spinning his web, waiting patiently until Roger was in so deep there was no way out. Roger was useful, able to give Arif something he had never had; a legitimate lawyer with an unblemished record, Jonathan Southern, who Arif used to full advantage. He relied on the fact that Roger's life was the only collateral that he needed to secure the services of this unassuming man. For, four years, Jonathan reluctantly covered Arif's illegal activities, finding inventive ways to cover Arif's tracks, being there as and when required to meet his every need. He witnessed beatings and much worse, things a human being had no right to see. Yet throughout, Roger continued to spiral out of control. There was no respect, nor love, for the father who had given up his own life to save him. He believed he was untouchable; that the rules did not apply to him. Then one day he went too far, committing the worst sin of all, stealing from Arif. Jonathan did his best to conceal it through imaginative accounting, but unbeknown to him, his son was being watched. Once again, Jonathan found himself begging for his son's life. While Arif promised he would allow him to speak to Roger, sort things out, repay the money, his son's sudden disappearance made it clear that. For Roger, there was no coming back.

"You think you've got nothing to lose, well, let me reassure you that is not the case. You are in too deep Jonathan; you have become an intrinsic part of all my wrongdoing. You my dear friend, have made it possible for me to move onto bigger and better things. Now I need that shipment to go through without any hitches and I need those papers to do it … so … where are they?"

Jonathan held firm, knowing that his life now hung by a thread and silence was his only protection. If only he had a chance to talk to Richard. He wondered if Richard had opened the envelope containing the transit documents. He had no way of knowing, because every attempt to contact Richard proved impossible throughout the week.

"Take him" Arif looked on, sat in his chair as Cassell and his men dragged Jonathan out the door.

"Arif, we do not have time for this!" Hussein was frustrated by the fact that they had made no headway. "Without those documents the deal is off."

"Calm down Hussein, help yourself to another drink, it really is the finest brandy."

Hussein headed for the door. "I've had enough of your games, when you're ready to deal with the big boys call me."

"I know where the documents are, he left them with Richard Templeton three days ago."

"Then why waste time with this charade?"

"I need to know if Southern talked, what he told this Templeton."

"Don't you think the place would be swarming with police if he had talked?"

"They're too smart for that, they want to catch me with the merchandise; without it they have nothing." Arif continued.

"What about Templeton?"

"It's all in hand."

"Arif I have no intention of walking into a trap. If this Templeton knows something we're all..."

"Hussein you really need to calm down, learn to trust me. Everyone has a price; you just have to find an incentive, the right carrot to dangle, by the time I've finished with Templeton he will tell me everything I need to know."

"Well if you've got an ace up your sleeve, I suggest you play it now, because we're running out of time and my clients won't wait."

Chapter 19

❦

Friday

I checked in with Joyce, as promised, and did my best to get her back on side but she thwarted my attempts and demanded to know who I was seeing. Even if I wanted to tell her, it would have served no purpose because now I knew about Charlotte, it would only be a matter of time before whatever Richard and I had ended, so what good would it do? The less she knew the better.

I had not seen Richard since we left each other at the Ritz. I know I should have been ready to hang, draw and quarter him but had resigned myself to the fact that our time was precious and I was not going to let anything spoil it. I had no idea where he was taking me, but knowing Richard, it was definitely going to be something I had never experienced before.

What made matters worse was Richard insisted on picking me up at the flat and he would not take no for an answer, which meant I spent most of the evening tidying up. I wondered what he would make of my humble abode. He probably had his own personal valet or something, but I was by no means ashamed of my place; I loved it and it was my home. I worked hard to pay the mortgage every month, which I somehow knew Richard would appreciate.

I was glad that I had taken Anna's advice to buy one pair of expensive shoes that must be black, as they would go with anything. I pulled out the shoebox containing my LK Bennett's, removed them carefully from the box and examined them. They set me back three hundred pounds; the most I had ever spent on any shoe I own. I suddenly thought about how this would be a flash in the pan for someone like Charlotte Hemmings, but quickly decided that if I stood a chance of getting through this evening I must take all my feelings for her and seal them away in an imaginary chest in the corner of my mind.

I was still in my robe when I heard the doorbell and panicked, as Richard was not due for another hour. On opening the door, a stone faced Anna barged past me and into the flat without saying hello.

"Oh come in why don't you." I said.

"I want to know everything! It's the least you can do after the grilling your sister has been giving me ... Oh my God, this dress is wicked."

I entered the front room to find Anna sizing the white dress up against her body in my living room mirror.

"You do know this is an original? OMG I cannot even begin to think how much this set him back. I'm not even going to ask … ok, tell me, how much did this set him back?"

"I didn't ask." I carefully removed the dress from Anna and returned it to my bedroom. Anna followed me in, sitting on the bed, intensely watching me apply the final touches to my make-up.

"Don't cake it on like you're plastering a ceiling, did I teach you nothing?" Anna grabbed the mascara. "You need those big brown eyes to pop out and you won't achieve that by submerging them in a slimy mess." Anna rubbed the end of the mascara applicator on the inside of the tube, getting rid of the excess. "I wish I'd brought my lash comb." She said.

"Anne you're making me nervous."

"Whatever," Anna replied as she continued to carefully apply the mascara. "I'm liking the foundation. Bobbie Brown may be a little expensive but it does the trick. Where's your brush?" She searched through my make-up bag until she found the large foundation brush and the pressed powder. I sat patiently and allowed her to dab the powder around the centre of my face, then blended it outwards. "See that's how you do it and you need a hint of blue on those lids." She was meticulous, taking extreme care with every detail.

"Thanks, that looks better." I was actually happy with the finished result.

"Praise indeed." Anna picked up the L K Bennetts. "I'm thinking we need to reassess the viability of these shoes."

"But they're the most expensive pair I've got."

"Pats, it's not about the price, it's about the look." Anna headed for the wardrobe and began searching through my very limited collection. "What do we have here? Tah Dah!" she said in excitement, as she handed me a pair of high-heeled silver shoes.

"I picked them up cheap in TK Maxx!"

"TK only deal in designer stuff, so you've got nothing to worry about. Give a girl the correct footwear and she can conquer the world." Anna had fun beautifying me, even insisting that I wear the Dolce & Gabbana perfume Joyce bought me for Christmas. She was indeed my fairy godmother. Finally, I was dressed and ready to go; I knew there was no turning back.

"You look different," said Anna

"That's hardly surprising, look at me!"

"I mean you, you're different ... you've fallen for him haven't you?"

It was pointless trying to pretend, and I was too tired to try.

"I can't remember what my life was like before he was in it. I can't remember how I felt, what I wanted."

"And how does he feel?" Anna asked. I suppose this would have been the perfect time to tell my best friend about Charlotte; tell her that this amazing man who had given me more in a few days than any man I had ever known, was deceitful, unfaithful and I had been complicit in enabling his behaviour. Yet, although it was on the tip of my tongue, I couldn't do it. I could not distort the illusion of perfection. I wanted to protect him, I used to ridicule women who would do anything to protect their man, defend them no matter what. I used to think they were stupid, naïve; God, love really is blind.

"He makes me feel like I'm the only woman in the world, Anna ... I sang for him."

"Jesus you must have been really tanked!" Anna adjusted the straps on my dress and made the final changes to my hair.

"I was a pissed as a fart" We both relaxed into laughter.

"Ok, so tell me again and remember, as your bestest friend in the world, you have no right to withhold this information."

"What?"

"How tall is he, what colour are his eyes and is he sexy?"

"Well I'm six two, my eyes are blue and I'd say in answer to your last question I think I'm bold enough to say I would pass as fairly sexy ... sorry the door was open, so I let myself in." Anna and I turned to find Richard standing behind us decked out in his Tuxedo. I must have left the door off the latch and, as usual,

Richard had taken full advantage of the element of surprise. Anna was lost for words.

"Hi I'm Richard, nice to meet you," Richard extended his hand to Anna; he was carrying a large bunch of yellow roses. He turned to me and smiled.

"You really are an amazing looking woman Patsy Cunningham, wouldn't you agree Anna?" Richard was overflowing with a smug kind of confidence.

"Yeah" I nudge Anna in the back. "Anyway I've got to be going, I've clearly outstayed my welcome..." said Anna not taking her eyes off Richard for a second while I hustled her out into the hall. Anna could hardly contain her excitement. "Are you twisted? He looks like James Bond! There is no way anyone in their right mind would ever let something like that go!"

"Bye Anna."

"You do realise I'm not going to get a wink of sleep until you call, so make sure you call! No matter how late, call me!" I agreed to call as I shuffled her out of the flat. As I shut the door, I felt Richard's arms around me. He pressed against me, pinning me to the door before impatiently wrapping his tongue around mine.

"Why Mr Templeton, anyone would think you've missed me." I said and pushed him away in order to catch my breath. "Welcome to my humble abode." I held his hand and carefully guided him back into the lounge to find the yellow roses lying on the table. Richard picked up the flowers and formally handed them to me.

"These are for you."

"Thank you, they're beautiful. I hope I've got a vase big enough to fit them in." I headed into the small kitchen, aware that Richard was close behind. "Would you like a drink?" I said nervously. "I've got some wine, Perrier and fruit juice."

"I'll have a Perrier please." I started hunting around for a large vase. I rarely get flowers so hardly ever use vases, but knew that someone had given me one as a flat warming present; where it was promptly discarded in the kitchen cupboard somewhere. God it would be so embarrassing if I could not find it, luckily, it was hidden behind the frying pan and the blender and it was thankfully made of pure clear glass, indicating that whoever bought it had taste.

I laid the vase next to the flowers on the kitchen sink and Richard stood by the small door watching while I pulled out the Perrier from the fridge.

"This is a nice flat Patsy."

"Why thank you! And it's all mine, well at least when I pay off the mortgage that is. Feel free to look around." Richard took his drink and disappeared into the flat. I hoped I had not left anything too embarrassing lying around.

After carefully arranging the flowers in the vase, I took them into the front room to find Richard looking at the various pictures of my family.

"Is this your sister?" he asked.

"Yes that's her."

"She looks like you."

"I know; she's five years older and she never lets me forget it."

"These are your parents?" There was an old black and white photograph of my mum and dad on the day of their wedding. Richard walked along thoroughly examining every photograph and I wondered if he would ever give me the opportunity to do the same in respect to his family.

"Do you have any brothers or sisters?" I asked, hoping he would not think it too much of an invasion of his privacy.

"No I'm an only child." Richard replied.

"Were you lonely?"

"At times, yes, but it wasn't all bad; when you spend a lot of time alone you become resourceful. I became very good at occupying myself which made me self-sufficient."

"You must have had friends." I said settling myself on the sofa as Richard talked about himself, something I had not expected.

"I had some good friends, people say it's harder to mix when you're an only child; I never experienced that, but I've never really had a close friend. Not like you have Anna. Rupert and I are close but it's not the same."

"Why didn't you go into medicine like your dad?"

"To be honest, the thought of cutting people open never really appealed to me." Richard unbuttoned his jacket and sat next to me.

"Why law?" I asked

"I could ask you the same question." Richard replied.

"I asked you first."

"The money; and I knew I'd be good at it. What about you?"

"I'd love to say it was about the money but as you've probably guessed I don't make very much, but even though it stresses me out I'm very lucky to do something I enjoy and I get the bonus of making my parents very proud."

"Your family are very important to you aren't they?" Richard gently stroked my face.

"Yes, but I don't know what they would make of my behaviour over the last few days." I whispered, losing my breath as he turned his attentions to my bare neck.

"Do you want us to stop Patsy?"

"Do you?" I was suddenly very scared.

"I asked you first."

"No I don't want us to stop."

"Well that's good to hear, because I couldn't let you go even if I wanted to." Richard pulled me towards him, kissing me passionately.

Chapter 20

After various failed attempts at trying to persuade Richard to tell me where we were going, I yielded and decided to enjoy the ride. We drove down long country roads and I was beginning to think we would never get to our destination, but after what seemed an age I saw bright lights ahead and as we turned into the large drive I was truly astonished at the sight before me. It was the most beautiful building I had ever seen, lit up like a Christmas tree. As Richard pulled up, a young man in uniform ran over and opened my door. This was too much, I had to pinch myself.

"Good evening Madam," said the enthusiastic young man who helped me out of Richard's grey and very classy M3 Sports BMW. I looked up in awe at the building and, as Richard joined me taking my arm, I saw the young man behind the wheel of the car taking it further down the drive and into a large car park.

"What do you think?" asked Richard.

"I get the feeling we're not in Kansas anymore." Richard laughed guiding me up the majestic steps. "Richard what is this place?"

"Wait and see."

As we entered, there was an array of tables with beautifully dressed people seated and standing around them. There were large machines dotted all over the room and the bustle of noise was all around us. Gorgeous, scantily dressed women walked around with trays of drinks.

"Oh my God we're in a Casino! Richard I've never been in a casino before, what do I do?"

"Let's start by having a drink."

We headed for the bar and Richard helped me to sit with finesse on the stool in my long dress. A tall barman greeted us.

"What can I get you Sir?"

I lean over to Richard and whisper. "I feel like ordering a Martini shaken and not stirred."

"Do you like Martinis?" whispered Richard.

"Never tried one before" I giggled.

"I'll have two dry white Martini's ... Shaken and not stirred." Said Richard in the worst Sean Connery accent I had ever heard.

"Coming up Sir" smiled the barman.

"I can't believe you just did that." I say sinking my head into Richard's arms.

"I'm sure I'm not the first and I won't be the last. Are you pleased with your surprise?"

"Richard I can't get my head around it, this place is amazing. You're not going to lose thousands of pounds are you?"

"No I'm not and why do you assume I'm going to lose?"

"Oh I don't know. In all the movies I see, people always lose."

"No, gambling's a mug's game; I've come here on the odd occasion and have a flutter here and there but no more than that. Would you like to have a go?"

"I'd love to but I wouldn't know how."

"Patsy you spent six years studying law, compared to that, this will be a piece of cake."

The barman returned with the drinks, placed them in front of us and Richard and I clinked glasses. The martini tasted crisp and slightly spicy, a pleasant taste that warmed my insides. I took another sip almost immediately.

"Take it easy," said Richard watching me intensely.

"Sorry, it tastes nice." Not at all concerned with how incredibly naïve I must have sounded. People were all around us, some watching, some playing. Richard took me to a small table with just two people and a dealer, who expertly shuffled cards, laying them on the table. It was all happening so quickly I could not, for the life of me, work out what was going on.

"That's Black Jack," said Richard so close to me making my stomach turn.

"Ok ... what's Black Jack?"

"The value of your cards must be twenty-one or as close to twenty-one as you can get. You play against the dealer; other players at the table are of no concern."

"So I need an ace and a ten to win."

"Exactly, or as close to that as possible, without the value of the cards going over 21." Richard then proceeded to give me a tour around the casino, some people seemed to be taking it all too seriously whilst others were having the times of their lives. Richard had reserved a table in the casino restaurant. We ordered the Lobster Thermidor. The creamy dish melted in my mouth and I don't think I had ever tasted anything so good. I could not believe it when Richard ordered Champagne to accompany the meal. Champagne twice in one week; I was most definitely living the high life. I felt decadent and probably should have been ashamed of acting in a bourgeois fashion, but for all I knew this could be the last night I would be with Richard and, when in Rome and all that. Richard was driving, so only had a small glass and even though it would have been nice to finish an entire bottle, I decided to switch to Perrier, but only after enjoying another glass, or two. Over dinner, we said very little, just looking at each other and smiling. There was intensity between us, warmth. Maybe it was the effects of the Champagne, or maybe it was something else. After dinner, we danced together in the casino lounge to Barry White's *Love Theme*, holding each other tightly. Richard stroked my hair, kissing me softly, showing an intimacy which was powerful, strong. I wondered if he made Charlotte feel the same, then quickly dispelled any thoughts of her from my mind.

The evening had been wonderful, everything I could have hoped for, but I could not help wishing that the best was yet to come. As Richard guided me back to our table I heard a group of people shouting. "What are they doing?" I asked.

"That's craps."

"Run that by me again."

"It's one of the more exciting games, really gets the adrenalin going."

"How do you play?"

"Ok ... In craps you are called the shooter and there are about forty different bets that can be made."

"It sounds complicated."

"It's easier than you think, Patsy; all you need to get started is to understand the basic Pass Line bet."

"Pass Line bet?"

"You place your bet on the Pass Line, which is mapped out on the table before the new shooter begins. If the shooter rolls a 7 or 11 you win, but if the shooter rolls a 2, 3 or 12 you lose."

Richard took me over to the craps table and we squeezed our way in to see what was happening. It was difficult to understand how adults get so excited over a few dice on a table but once I got into the furore of it all, it was difficult not to feel the same. There was a large woman at the table who appeared to be winning, but I did not know enough about the game to be sure.

Richard put his arms around me and started to explain the rudiments of the game again.

"Right she's just thrown a seven and won and that means that everyone who placed a bet wins too." I watched as the dealer at the table paid out three or four people.

"How much do they win?"

"It depends on how much they put down. Look someone has put twenty pounds on the table so that twenty pounds is exchanged for chips and, as you can see, they are giving him small denominations of one pound and five pounds, which allow him to bet as much, or as little as he likes at a time. You see that black marker? That means that the table is open for bets, when it is turned over to white, the table is closed."

The woman and her friends screamed at the tops of their lungs, along with the rest of the table.

"She's on a winning streak and that means everyone else is." I looked at the chips in front of the woman and she had a number of different colours in front of her.

"How much do you think she has?" I asked watching as the woman rolled some chips in her hand.

"There's over five hundred pounds there," said Richard. "She should quit while she's ahead."

"No she shouldn't; couldn't she make just one big bet and double her money."

"She could bet any seven but that's a high risk bet and it's a one roller, which means you get one chance; it's a shot in the dark, a wish and a prayer."

"I'd do it."

"Patsy you'd be every casino owner's dream; they bank on people like you making high-risk bets."

"I still think she should do it. She's having the time of her life. If she goes out, it should be on a high not a low. Besides, it will show she's got guts; anyone can be good at something, but not everyone's lucky and it looks like tonight's her night, so this is as good a time as any."

"Babes, you know you make a lot of sense." Neither Richard nor I were aware that the woman throwing the dice had been privy to our conversation. "This gorgeous young woman here thinks I should go for it, what do you think people?"

The entire table cheered.

"Patsy Cunningham, I can't take you anywhere" said Richard.

"How was I supposed to know she was listening?"

"Come over 'ere darling, give me some moral support and bring that handsome young man with ya an' all."

Richard and I were pulled towards the woman at the front of the table. God what have I done? Me and my big mouth.

"If she loses I'll never forgive myself." I said to Richard over all the noise.

"It's her decision, not yours," replied Richard shouting over everyone.

I was dismayed to see the woman pick up all the chips in front of her.

"Wait a minute, maybe you should think this through." I was definitely having second thoughts.

"Listen darling it's only money. I've been on this table for hours and I ain't lost yet. What you lose today you get back tomorrow and anyway, it's like you said, I'm on a roll. Can I have silence please?" The table went deadly silent and I sank my head into Richard's arms as I could not look. I was having such a good time and I had to go and spoil it. The woman tossed all her chips towards the dealer and said "any seven please" and the dealer placed the bet. I heard the sighs from around the table as everyone recognised that there was no going back as the dealer turned the black marker over to white, closing the table. I heard the shaking of the dice and felt sick. I looked up to watch the woman expertly toss them across to the far side of the craps table with everyone transfixed as the dice seemed to turn over and over again before finally settling themselves on … the lucky number seven. A feeling of elation took hold of the entire room with me slap in the middle of it. The woman clung to me kissing and hugging me as if we were long lost relatives;

she had won over a thousand pounds. The exhilaration experienced through winning was amazing, and I did not even place a bet. I tried to get to Richard but there was now a sea of people between us. It had been the best night of my life. Oh God if only this could last forever.

Chapter 21

I slept most of the way home, only waking up when we were just a few streets away. Richard looked tired and I was not sure whether I should ask him in once he pulled up outside the flat.

"Richard I want to thank you for giving me one the best nights of my entire life."

"The pleasure was all mine; it's been an eventful week." Richard turned off the engine.

"That's putting it mildly. I'd offer you a coffee but the truth is I don't keep any in the house. I love the smell but hate the taste, but I do have tea."

"Well in that case I'd love a cup of tea." Richard in his usually gallant fashion opened my door and helped me out of the car. The flat was chilly, so I lit the gas flamed fire in the lounge on my way to the kitchen. It was the best feature of the room.

"Why don't you put some music on?" I shouted from the kitchen as I filled the kettle. I returned to find Richard going through my various CD's and was pleased when he chose the best of Randy Crawford.

"Wasn't it great when she won? I don't know what I would have done if she hadn't."

"Patsy, you never cease to amaze me."

"Why?"

"You embrace everything so completely," said Richard.

"I didn't even make a bet."

"You didn't need to" Richard replied.

"I envy people who can do something like that, throw all their chips on the table and to hell with the consequences. It was easy for me to say; I wasn't taking the risk, but when she threw those dice my heart was pounding and when she won it was brilliant! I'll make the tea."

"Leave the tea and come here." Randy Crawford's *Endlessly* began to play and I knew how I wanted the night to end. I was glad when it became clear that Richard wanted the same. I ran my fingers through his thick, dark hair and our tongues impatiently danced with one another. His lips were wet and soft, I nipped the top of them ever so gently as he cupped my face in his hands.

"There's something I haven't told you, something you need to know" said Richard. I was suddenly afraid that he was going to confess. I should have wanted him to tell me the truth, yet I did not want anything to spoil this moment. Right now, I only wanted it to be about him and me. Her intrusion and any reference to his affinity and feelings towards her were not welcome. I placed my hands on his lips summoning his silence. Richard drew down the zip on the back of my dress, wasting no time in unclasping my strapless bra, gently holding my breasts in his hands; he hungrily sucked on my pert and alert nipples, forcefully turning my back to towards him, wrenching my thong away. I could feel him rubbing against my cheeks, searching for my inner sanctum. He was rough but this didn't scare me; I just wanted him inside me and as he plunged in I screamed in pain and pleasure. I wanted him to hurt me, I wanted to experience the complete power that he would bring, thrusting into me me hard and strong from behind as he pinned me against the wall.

"I can't stop thinking about you; you're on my mind every minute of the day." Richard moaned as he continued his rhythm.

"Stay with me tonight." I groaned as Richard pulled out and we made our way towards the bedroom, before we removed the rest of our clothing, Richard reached into the inside pocket of his Tux and pulled out a small red tube.

"What's that?" I asked

"Don't worry…it's a surprise." As I did not wish to spoil the moment, I said no more. We lay on the bed kissing and caressing every inch of our naked bodies, but it wasn't enough. I wanted more; I needed to be taken to another level, to feel his mouth on me and mine wrapped around him; and this was the time. I manoeuvred myself, hovering over Richard, my round arse pointed towards his face. My wet interior lowered towards his waiting lips whilst my salacious tongue dropped into place to wrap itself around his juicy penis. I could taste myself on him and shivered as Richard teased my opening with the tip of his tongue, before burrowing his way deeply within my gateway. In turn, I entangled my succulent tongue, enmeshing it around his upright rod. As he tunnelled further down he clutched my curved arse and I writhed in response. We suckled each other impatiently and our nectars flowed as we revelled in immense pleasure. I was a sea of juices, receptive and willing to his every touch. Have you ever been so absolutely content that you do not want the moment to end? For me, my thoughts could only be compared to gorging on the most delectable chocolate fudge brownie with a silky Belgian chocolate centre running through it, just waiting for my spoon to cut into it and release ripples of sweetness. The thing is, as you bite into the brownie and the gorgeous, amazing taste trickles and tingles down the side of your mouth, you know it's bad for you, dangerous, but your willpower is gone; any hope of abstaining no longer exists. Therefore, you give in to its taste and the sheer exhilaration of it.

Richard suddenly pulled himself from under me, delicately running his fingers down my naked body.

I lay flat on my stomach, shivered as the tips of his fingers worked their magic along my spine, he nipped at my ear first one then the other and I leaned my head back into his arms and he encased me with his legs, which I felt tighten around me. It was then that I felt his fingers begin to massage my back passage, a forbidden place that I have never allowed any man to enter.

"Richard, I can't, I've never…"

"I want to be in every part of you, Patsy … let me in."

"But it's going to hurt."

"Relax, just relax, let yourself go Patsy, give yourself completely to me." whispered Richard as he continued to stroke my buttocks. The stimulation was insurmountable. I could feel his fingers feeling the way; I arched as he prodded at my forbidden passage, it was then I smelt the strong smell of strawberries and the cold sensation of the lubricant being gently massaged into me. I was scared but also excited at the thought of taking the first steps into an unknown realm and he only began to push his penis into me when he knew I was ready to receive it. At first, it was painful and I winced in agony, but Richard was so soothing and took his time and the emollient helped to ease the way.

"It's alright baby, I won't hurt you, I just want to love you, let me in; that's it baby … just relax completely and let me in."

Richard's soft voice and the beautiful smell of strawberries, which filled the room, enabled me to calm down and as I relaxed, he gave a firm thrust and was inside me. He was so careful, keeping his crusade to slow strides. I felt him pressed into my back and heard his groans of pleasure.

"You're so tight, so beautifully tight." He moaned as he began to move a little faster. I thought I would hate it, yet, being so constricted made his intrusion more intense, only increasing the sensation. Richard did not disappoint as he continued to thrust on and on, with each stride he delved deeper and deeper, he used his fingers as he began to search for the other opening within me, which was now so wet that I felt his fingers slip and slide. He was tender, patient and on finding my clitoris, that jewel within me, he began to work his magic, using the tips of his fingers; teasing me into complete and utter submission whilst continuing to drive his hardened Penis into me from behind. I allowed myself to descend into a state of ecstasy. I could feel my volcano beginning to erupt like boiling lava as he once again manipulated my body to his will. I was lost and it was at that moment that we became one, imploding into each other with the essence of our flowing juices.

Saturday

It was eight a clock in the morning and as Richard made his way to the door, I held onto the tail of his jacket like a child being left by her mother on her first day at school. I didn't want to let him go. Before opening the door, he turned to me, wrapping his arms around me and I snuggled up against him.

"Why can't you stay?" I heard myself asking.

"Don't make this harder for me than it is already Patsy."

"I want to make it hard for you because I don't want you to leave me." I was beginning to sound desperate but I didn't care, besides I couldn't bear the thought of him leaving me and going to her. As Richard turned to open the door, I felt a pain in the pit of my stomach and tried to hold back the tears but was unsuccessful. He held my face in his hands and kissed my forehead wiping my tears away.

"Patsy do you believe me when I tell you I've never wanted anyone as much as I want you?" I nod in agreement. "And no matter what happens, that's never going to change." I wanted to believe him, but how could I, knowing that he was leaving me and going to her. The night somehow made it easier to put those feelings away, but the cold light of day had put everything back into a horrible perspective. I hated being second best, hated not being the one, but in spite of that and as we kissed and caressed each other at my open door, all I could think of was how long it would be until we would see each other again.

Chapter 22

"Is that him?" Joyce asked Anna as they watched Richard fiddle for the keys to his sporty BMW.

"Yeah that's him." Anna replied, sitting in the front seat of Joyce's car.

"Are you sure that's him?

"Joyce, I could hardly mistake him now could I?"

"Wait here." said Joyce.

"Patsy isn't going to like this."

"Then don't tell her."

Anna nervously looked on as Joyce walked over to Richard, praying that Patsy would never find out she had betrayed her. Joyce was relentless, turning up at her flat in the early hours, badgering her until she got the answers she wanted. Joyce had always been over protective of Patsy, but it was not until now that Anna realised just how far she was prepared to go. She spent most of the night trying to reason with Joyce, to get her to understand that Patsy was her own woman with the right to make her own choices. What was so wrong about her wanting nice things or to be taken to nice places? Yet, Anna recognised that this theory could easily be applied to someone who was only interested in what they could get; someone who did not care about consequences. She knew her friend was different. She saw a look in Patsy's eyes yesterday that made it clear that she was falling deeper and deeper under the spell of Richard Templeton and regretted telling her to throw caution to the wind. She pondered her betrayal, but justified it by looking back at how hard it had been for Patsy, how much she had already endured, after having to find her back from the most terrifying experience, in which she was at the mercy of an obsession, which left her guarded and afraid. She had come so far, achieved so much and Joyce was right, if Richard did not intend to take the relationship to the next level it was best that she find out now.

As Joyce approached Richard in his now somewhat dishevelled Tux, wearing his morning stubble, she could understand how her sister could have been taken in so quickly. He was beautiful.

"I want a word with you." said Joyce.

"I'm sorry do I know you?"

"I'm Joyce, Patsy's sister. I need to talk to you."

This was all Richard needed. His brain was doing cartwheels as it was, and his feelings, which were usually under control, were erratic to say the least, but he could see that Joyce was not about to be fobbed off.

"God, you do look alike." Richard was unnerved by the resemblance.

"We'll talk in the car shall we?" Joyce opened the passenger door and got in without waiting for a response. "Nice vehicle, cost you a lot did it?"

"A fair amount."

"You used to having nice things?"

"I work hard, have a comfortable life yes ... I know what you're thinking."

"Do you? Then tell me Mr Templeton, what am I thinking?" Joyce's tone was hard and cold, but deep down in her heart she prayed that Richard would provide her with the answer she so badly wanted; that he cared for her sister, wanted to be with her, make her happy. May be then Joyce could finally rid herself of the guilt that had gripped her so long.

"Look Patsy's special, I care about her."

"Oh she's so special and you care so much that you sneak around to see her." Nothing was coming out the way that Joyce intended.

"Listen..."

"No you listen. You haven't got a clue what Patsy's been through to get to where she is now."

"What do you mean?" asked Richard. Joyce realised that she had said too much.

"All you need to know is I care about my sister, I know her better than she knows herself; and looking at you, I have no doubt in my mind that she's already fallen head over of heels, which means it's too late for her not to get hurt in all this. But, it is still not too late for her to get over it if you walk away. The funny thing is, even though I want to rip your head off right now, I've got this gut feeling that you really care about her. I don't think you planned this, I don't believe either of you did, but Richard I'm asking you, begging you, if you have not been completely honest with her or don't want a future with Patsy ... end it now."

"Patsy's a grown woman with the right to make her own choices."

"Oh so let me get this right, you've chosen her have you? You want to be with my sister, you intend to give everything up to be with her ... that's precisely why you're sneaking out of her flat in the early hours of the morning when no one can see you. Listen, if you really care about her, I know you would want her to be happy, with someone who can give her what she needs. If that's you then great. But I get the feeling it's not."

Richard rested his head on the steering wheel, taking in Joyce's words, wondering how so much could happen in one week.

Joyce left Richard alone in the car with his thoughts.

"What happened?" said Anna eager to find out what had happened. Joyce did not respond. "What did you say to him?"

"What needed saying."

"Joyce I'm not sure about this. I only met him for a little while but I think he really likes her." Joyce chose not to tell Anna she believed her, having said the same thing to Richard just a few minutes before, but none of that changed the fact that Richard clearly did not intend to make a life with Patsy.

"Like is not love, like is not a home and a family which is what my sister deserves."

As Joyce drove Anna home, she could not help thinking that maybe she had gone too far. Did she have the right to interfere in Patsy's life, making demands, giving ultimatums? If Patsy ever found out, would she ever forgive her? Suddenly there was a twinge of regret, but only a twinge.

Chapter 23

Joyce's words resonated through Richard, leaving him very unsettled. On the one hand, he was angry that she had accosted him in that way, making demands. She had no right. On the other hand, he knew that she was only acting out of love for Patsy, which, he could not deny, was commendable. Joyce saw him as a selfish man, using his money to manipulate Patsy, but was Patsy any different? She had accepted all his gifts and played along. He never made any promises, never told her this was forever.

He was a successful businessman with a flourishing legal practice, which he had worked hard to build, and he had allowed sentiment, passion to place that in jeopardy. He could not risk any scandal, Joyce was right about him caring for Patsy and he was glad that at least she recognised this in him. He was not being fair, he remembered as Patsy clung to him that morning that, for her, it had gone to next level. Everything had happened so quickly; it had spiralled out of control. It was time to step back, take stock, think about what was best for both he and Patsy. He had no choice but to give Patsy up, walk away. It did not matter that she was the first thing he thought of in his waking hour and the last thing he thought of before closing his eyes at night. It did not matter that the thought of her naked body next to him made him shudder in excitement and every moment spent with her would be cherished for the rest of his life. None of that mattered because now he needed to be cold, calculating. He viewed this episode as a blip, an error of judgement on his part, one last fling before he settled down with his perfect wife and two point four children somewhere deep in suburbia. It was over.

Chapter 24

✤

Hussein prepared himself for his meeting with Arif, cleaning his Colt Defender, carrying its three barrels with a precision that could have only have been achieved through years of practice. With its lightened trigger, the gun had become his pride and joy, saving his life as well as taking others with considerable accuracy. Loading the seven round magazines and carefully hiding it away within its holster inside his jacket was the final stage in the process.

Hussein was used to being in a lonely place, detaching himself from the world and the people within it. He had spent the last ten years of his life living in and out of hotel rooms, never being in one place for long enough to be discovered. As the years moved on, it had become more difficult for him to distinguish between the job he had been paid to do and the real world. He had no wife, no children; it was safer that way. Yet, living in complete isolation had serious pitfalls.

He was becoming more stressed, more prone to anxiety brought on by the unpredictability of living from day to day not knowing whether it would be his last. There were no controls or checks to keep him in place, so in order to maintain the illusion of stability he cut off all fragments of emotion, becoming empty and uncaring, which helped to keep him alive, only giving in to his imperfection once the job was done. He did not need to addict himself to drugs or alcohol, something he had watched so many others do. His only objective was to stay alive long enough to move onto the next big deal, which would only have been more difficult if he had to rely on stringing himself up into the oblivion of being on a high, or needed a drink to get through each day. He had to keep his wits about him and was doing it the only way he knew how.

He had changed his identity so many times it had become second nature to him, with cropped black hair and deep blue eyes he looked older than his thirty-seven years. For the first time, the lines were becoming blurred. He was beginning to forget who he really was, not surprising as he was deeper than he had ever been before.

He drove towards the gates of the large warehouse and waited as one of Arif's men opened them, securing them once he was on the other side. Every meeting carried its own risk, but Arif trusted him. Hussein was the courier, the link between Arif and Hussein's clients and if he failed, it all failed.

Hussein had been working on this deal for nearly two years, with Arif being the final piece of the puzzle.

Arif was hungry for success, for the accolades that this would bring. The money, although considerable, was not the driving force; it was the power that it would reel to Arif if it was successful. It would take him onto the international stage, what he had been waiting for all his life. Like most people blinded by greed and power, Arif was prepared to risk everything. However, he was entering into a world he did not understand and because of that, he made mistakes. When making deals of this nature you needed people around you that could be trusted, people with a backbone who would not fall into a quivering wreck at the first sign of trouble. The crooked lawyers used by Arif for his petty crime and gambling outlets were sufficiently qualified to deal with that, but not this. They had neither the nous nor the business acumen that Arif required; most importantly they had no pull, no reputation behind them that would give the clients on the other side of the Atlantic the confidence in Arif that he badly craved.

Concealing the consignment was, of course, the crucial element of the deal and even though Arif had a person on the inside within customs, they could not secure success without the authentic legal documents required that would accompany the precious artifacts that would conceal the consignment. When shipping items abroad no one can escape bureaucracy. Hussein had underestimated Arif, who had a plethora of contacts that were more useful to him than he could have imagined.

Hussein watched as Arif's men carefully removed the diamonds from their deep blue velvet casings, he followed them to a table, which contained two large and skillfully fashioned statues. One made of marble the other of bronze with an immaculate finish. They would both stand within the finest of interiors or collections, authentic to the eye, cold to the touch. Hussein examined the marble bust made in the guise of the Roman Emperor Caesar and carefully pulled a tiny lever concealed within the sculptured crown, which opened to reveal a hollow shell containing two compartments, and then he carefully lowered the diamonds inside. He placed the uncut stones into the compartment, pressed the lever, which closed the crown back into place.

"Ingenious" said Arif very impressed.

"I have arranged for one hundred of these figurines to be brought to you tonight. When will you have the full delivery?" Hussein asked, not bothering to acknowledge the compliment.

"By tonight, it's ready and waiting to be shipped" Arif was confident.

"And the documents?"

"That's all in hand."

"How?"

"Let me take care of that."

"You're making me nervous, Arif, and if I'm nervous so are my clients. If this deal fails…"

"It won't fail, trust me."

"One thing you learn in this business is to never trust anyone. Make it happen Arif, or we will all suffer the consequences."

Hussein made a final check of the merchandise and left, not looking back. Arif waited for him to drive away before summoning Cassell.

"Cassell, get Harvey. Bring him to me and clean up, you've got a party to attend."

Chapter 25

The drive to Richmond was gruelling. Having set off in the late afternoon in heavy traffic it took Richard a lot longer than he had anticipated to arrive. In addition, he could not shake the feeling of guilt that had settled on him. He still believed that he had made the right decision, that Patsy and he could never work and that his life was with Charlotte, but should he tell Charlotte about Patsy or not? How could he start a life with someone that began with a lie yet, what purpose would it serve to tell her? Charlotte would be the first to admit that they had grown apart but this was more Richard's fault than hers. With his busy work schedules and constant travelling. Now he was a changed man, the moment of madness was over and he had resigned himself to taking the easy road rather than one filled with the uncertainty that Patsy would bring. Joyce and Anna would look after her and in time, she would forget him.

Richard pulled up outside Richmond Mansion observing the beautiful people sipping their grey goose vodka and champagne cocktails, oblivious to his pain, and for one split second returned to the man he had become with Patsy. For five days, he was able to shed the shackles of inhibition which had limited the real Richard Templeton, who he was reluctant to supress again. In his world, however, people were required to behave in a certain fashion, they said and did the right things at all times and maintained a level of decorum befitting their lifestyle.

Patsy was far away from that world. Unlike the people he now so closely scrutinised, she fought for her position in life, not expecting anything from anyone, living with an honesty that most of them could only dream of. Even if he lost all reason and sanity failed to prevail, he could not subject her to this materialistic world and consequential recrimination.

"Oh my God, it's Mr Templeton, we are honoured." Isabella was loud and obnoxious, and a little inebriated.

"Hello Isabella," Richard, slowly got out of the car "Happy Birthday."

"Don't I get a birthday kiss?" Isabella said as she draped herself around him. Richard steadied Isabella on her feet and was taken by surprise as she planted a sloppy kiss on his lips.

"Why didn't I see you first? You are literally sex on legs." Richard found himself going a little red but, being the perfect gentleman, passed Isabella carefully to one of her friends and made his way inside without responding.

"Richard there you are, I thought you'd never get here." Charlotte said as he rushed over carrying a large bottle of champagne.

"Charlotte we need to talk."

"Of course darling, but first I have the biggest surprise."

"Can't it wait?"

"No it can't wait." Charlotte, eagerly dragged Richard by the hand, leading him towards the library at the back of the Mansion. They squeezed through various groups of people with Charlotte stopping and kissing each and every one on her way, eventually disposing of the bottle of Champagne by leaving it in the hands of a welcome receiver who put the bottle to his head. As they got closer to the library, the kerfuffle died down and Charlotte turned to Richard, fixing his tie, which was already in place. She quietly knocked on the door and pushed it open.

"Daddy I've found him."

"Ah the elusive Mr Templeton, please Richard, come in." Randolph Hemmings rose to his feet to greet a bemused Richard, who had no idea why he had been summoned. Maybe he knew, had found out about his exploits. There were three other men in the large library filled with books, which probably had never been read, with a blazing fire as the centrepiece. Richard suddenly remembered the fireplace at Patsy's which was not as grand but somehow seemed a lot more welcoming.

"Please Richard sit." Said Randolph pointing to an armchair, the chair looked comfortable in front of the fire and all Richard wanted to do was collapse into it and sleep for a week but instead politely obeyed.

"That will be all Charlotte"

"But daddy…"

"We're going to talk shop. It will only bore you to death so go and make merry with your friends. Richard will find you when we have concluded our chat."

Charlotte blew Richard a kiss before leaving which he accepted with a smile. She quietly closed the door behind her leaving Richard to his fate.

"Richard, can I get you a drink?"

"No thank you Sir," Richard surveyed the formidable character before him, commanding respect.

"Can I introduce Michael Manders, Phillip Delaware and Anthony Hillman? They all have substantial holdings within my company" Richard acknowledged all three men who made him feel as if he were about to face the interview of his life. "Tell me Richard, what do you know about Formulie Enterprises?"

"Well Sir, it's a business you founded almost thirty years ago. You started it alone, using the inheritance of your late father to set up a number of property investments in areas, which included Canary Wharf, as well as in the City. You also obtained planning permission to redevelop areas singled out for regeneration, which allowed you to resell with that permission attached for a very healthy profit. The company now has a number of off-shore assets and you have various franchises throughout the world in hotels ranging from five to six stars. In a nutshell Formulie Enterprises has become one of the leading companies on, as well as off, British shores."

"Didn't I tell you this boy was impressive?" Randolph turned to the three men who all nodded in agreement. Randolph picked up a large class of whisky and took a sip before sitting down next to the other three men. Richard waited patiently but was keen to find out where this would lead.

"Richard my partners and I have been watching you for some time. You've built up a lucrative business and are an excellent barrister as well as an astute businessman; you're also young and you're hungry. How would you feel if we were to offer you the opportunity to take the helm within the Legal department for Formulie? You'd be responsible for overseeing my off-shore deals as well as taking care of domestic matters here."

"But I have a business."

"A business that can run itself. Richard the work you do now, you choose to do. You have a competent partner and a thriving business which allows you to do as much or as little as you like. I'm giving you the opportunity to become a leading executive in one of the biggest corporations in the world, and if you're as brilliant as I think you are you can go on to spearhead that company." Richard could not believe what he was hearing. He had never been given any indication that this was in the cards but realised that Charlotte's father must have been planning this for a while. It now all made sense; those meaningful philosophical chats held in his study, Randolph's extensive questions relating to his business, it was really an evaluation of his capabilities and clearly he had met the challenge. Could this be happening, today of all days? Richard could not deny this was the culmination of all his dreams.

"I don't need to tell you what this could mean to you." Randolph continued.

"But why me? I'm sure you have any number of protégés that could take on this role."

"But they are not you; you have intellect, business acumen, two crucial characteristics which could only be an asset to a corporation of this size."

"And I suppose Charlotte has nothing to with my intellect?" Richard decided this would not be the time to hold back.

"I admire your directness. I won't deny that I would be the last one to shed a tear if you also became my son-in-law. It seems the natural course of things, but it's not the determining factor, I can promise you that." Randolph was clever, thought Richard, knowing full well that it would be impossible to separate the two as one would most definitely lead to the other. "Of course it's far too big a decision to decide now, but Richard if you accept, it will change your life. I want you to know, this is not a decision that has been made lightly; I have invested a lot of time in finding out what makes you tick Richard. I know you are a man that loves a challenge; and that's what makes you perfect for Formulie ... Anyway enough shop talk, I'm sure my daughter is growing inpatient for your company." Richard rose with all four men, shaking each of their hands.

"Thank you for the opportunity and I promise you I will give your most generous offer serious consideration and would like to thank you for your faith in me Sir."

Charlotte was waiting anxiously outside and hugged Richard, unable to control her enthusiasm.

"Richard isn't it simply wonderful?"

"Did you have a hand in this?"

"I was just as surprised as you were when daddy told me his plans, which was only this afternoon, I swear. Didn't I always say you were brilliant? Do you know what this means? You could end up heading daddy's entire company."

"It sounds too good to be true."

"Well it is true. Richard. Just think, you won't have to worry about that silly little business of yours anymore, not with this behind you."

"Charlotte I'm a barrister first and foremost and I'm not sure I want to give that up. Rupert and I built my business from scratch and to walk away from it now…"

"You're not walking away, you are moving onto bigger and better things. Don't you see, this is a chance to make something of yourself."

"I thought I had."

"Well of course you have darling, but it's hardly on the same scale now is it?"

"If I take it, I suppose we'd have to get married," said Richard waiting for Charlotte's reaction.

"Well don't sound so enthusiastic about it. I was hoping you would want to marry me."

"Of course I do, it's the natural way of things after all." Charlotte embraced Richard as they kissed for the first time that night, but as they held each other, Richard did not feel right. In spite of the enormity of the offer, he could not help thinking that something or someone was missing. He pulled away from Charlotte.

"Richard what is it?"

"Charlotte there's something I need to tell you and I want you to know I never meant to hurt you."

"Richard what are you talking about? Has this got anything to do with how strange you've been acting over the last few days, don't you see? Nothing matters anymore, because with daddy behind us we are going to be rich beyond our wildest dreams!"

"Charlotte if we get married, I'm not going to be a puppet for your father. I need to be my own man."

"And you will be."

"I'll make my own money and my own rules."

"Oh Richard, aren't you being a little ungrateful? There you are being offered the opportunity of a lifetime and all you can think of is your independence."

"Tell me Charlotte, if I lost everything became penniless what would you do?"

"Oh now you're just being silly."

"Charlotte. What would you do?" Charlotte thought long and hard and Richard hoped that she would provide him with the answer he was hoping for, that she would stand by him no matter what and she would help him to rebuild his life.

"Richard, you know that daddy would never allow anything like that to happen. Goodness all this pessimistic talk is making me depressed and we're missing the party, come on we should be celebrating."

"I hope those celebrations include me" said Harvey who appeared from nowhere.

"Harvey!" screamed Charlotte jumping into Harvey's arms who responded by swinging her around. "Where have you been?"

"Holding up Isabella for the last half hour. The last time I saw her she was disappearing into the ladies room and I think she's in need of assistance as she has failed to resurface."

"I'd better go and rescue her. Harvey, keep Richard company will you until I get back? Under no circumstances let him drone on about being penniless. Get him a drink which will hopefully lighten his mood." Charlotte kissed Richard on the cheek as she rushed away to find Isabella.

"Forgive me for saying this, but you don't seem in the mood for a party. How about we find somewhere a little less chaotic?" said Harvey as he pointed Richard towards some stairs leading to the lower floor.

"I'll take you up on that." Richard replied as Harvey led him away, not noticing the two men following them as they disappeared down the back stairs.

* * *

Richard collapsed on the long sofa in the small room at the far side of the Mansion and Harvey looked on, helping himself to a drink.

"You look done in dear boy. Here have a drink." said Harvey, handing Richard a glass of brandy, which Richard took with appreciation.

"You're a Godsend Harvey" Richard finished the drink in one gulp.

"Can I get you another?"

"No that hit the spot thanks." Richard lay flat on the sofa and Harvey moved around to the back of him.

"I'm glad I've got you alone Richard, there's something I've been meaning to talk to you about."

"Harvey I don't mean to be rude but can it wait? I don't think I can take anything else in tonight. I just need some shut eye."

"I'm sorry Richard I'm afraid it can't wait, you see I have a problem that I need you to help me with."

"What kind of a problem?" said Richard, his hands covering his forehead.

"I've got myself into a spot of bother and the only way I get myself out of it is if you come with me now." Richard sits up.

"Come with you … what are you talking about?"

"Believe me Richard it would be better for all of us if you don't ask any questions and do as I ask."

"For God's sake Harvey, I have no intention of going anywhere with you."

"I was hoping we could do this without any unpleasantness but you seem intent on making things difficult." Harvey opened the door, allowing Cassell and his men to enter.

"Harvey what the hell is going on?"

"He's all yours." The men approached Richard who, by now had jumped off the sofa and backed against the wall. Richard was determined to put up a fight and managed to knock one of the men to the floor.

"Do you want to bring the whole house down on us? Keep him quiet." said Harvey, cowering by the door. Before Richard had a chance to get away, Cassell gave him a hard blow to the stomach, sending him to the floor breathless, in excruciating pain. Cassell and his men dragged Richard to his feet, holding him down and covering his face with a dose of chloroform. Richard attempted to struggle but was knocked out almost immediately and was taken to a waiting car, out of sight at the rear of the Mansion, whilst Harvey kept watch before joining them.

Chapter 26

Hussein was not prepared for Arif's last minute changes, expecting the delivery of the diamonds to be made at the warehouse. The abandoned farmhouse was in a perfect location, hidden away in the depths of the countryside, allowing the shipment to be transported through hidden country lanes. It also afforded the advantage of an unrestricted view, making it virtually impossible for anyone to penetrate his defences without detection.

Hussein entered the cluttered kitchen, greeted by a smell of musty air and a hive of activity. Arif sat at a dusty table wrapped in a thick coat with two men at the door and two on either side of him as he smoked a large cigar. Hussein was nervous but had been in the business long enough to learn how to conceal it.

"I don't like last minute changes, Arif." The where-abouts of the diamonds had not been revealed and he was careful not to press Arif until the time was right. Now the time was right. "Where are the diamonds?"

"Patience Hussein, the truck is loaded. All we need to do is add the final busts which will contain the diamonds, which will be strategically placed within the legitimate goods."

"I've kept my end of the bargain, now it's your turn. Show me the merchandise or the deal is off."

"I think you've waited long enough," says Arif and nodded to Cassell who obediently laid a small attaché case on the table opened it and stood back.

"May I?" asked Hussein

"Be my guest." The case glittered as the plethora of diamonds glared at him. Hussein took a loupe from his top pocket and carefully began examining the stones, searching for small naturally occurring imperfections, in the guise of tiny flecks of minerals and very light colour changes. He tested a number of the pieces and each met with his approval, which proved they were the real thing. "Well Arif it looks like we're in business."

"My men will load the diamonds into the secret compartments."

"If it's all the same to you, I'll take care of that myself."

"Hussein has anyone ever told you, you have serious trust issues?" Hussein ignored the sarcasm as he carefully removed a handful of the precious stones and placed them in the first of the five open busts lying on the table, before sealing the lever down into place and carefully storing the bust in a box marked fragile.

"This is just the start, there's plenty more where these came from. Just think, a few more runs like this, Hussein, and we'll all be able to write our own ticket. Hell, you could even retire. I can see it now, you cuddled up before a large fireplace with your pipe and slippers."

"Don't be too hasty, we're not out of the woods yet, even with my man on the inside we're lost without those transit certificates. What if Southern talked? We could still be walking into a trap." Hussein continued examining the diamonds before safely securing them away in their hiding place.

The farmhouse door burst open as a semi-conscious Richard was dragged towards a waiting chair, groggy from the effects of the drug. Hussein showed no interest, conscious that time was precious.

"Wakey wakey, rise and shine Mr Templeton." Shouted Arif who beckoned his men to rouse Richard, which they did, slapping him hard in the face. Richard slowly came around, through distorted vision he tried to come to grips with his unfamiliar surroundings. He and Hussein gave each other a glancing look as Richard focused on the handful of diamonds being hidden away in the large busts.

"Welcome Mr Templeton, it's nice to finally meet you." said Arif.

"Where the hell am I? What is this?" said Richard holding his thumping head.

"There's no need to worry Richard, we're all friends here." replied Arif, as Richard tried to get his bearings.

"You seem to have me at a disadvantage." Richard's words were slurred and his head was pounding. Hussein looked on, curious as to how Arif intended to get the information he wanted.

"I'm a little hurt, I was sitting but a few tables away from you not two days ago. Your delightful fiancé joined us while you tucked into Caesar Salad, I believe."

"Oh yes, Harvey's associate. By the way, where is the treacherous little snake?"

"There's no love lost between the two of you is there? What did he call you? Ah yes, an arrogant little shit, were his exact words."

"Praise indeed." Richard retorted.

"You don't need to worry about the likes of Harvey, he scuttled off as soon as he was paid, lacks the stomach for this sort of thing."

"Although I find this banter between us riveting, I would appreciate it if you could get to the point."

"I admire your candour Mr Templeton." Arif leaned towards him. "Typical man of the law, going straight for the jugular." Arif threw a large brown envelope onto the table. Richard eyed the envelope suspiciously, reading the address scrawled across in bold black letters: **Jonathan Southern Associates, 25 Pennington Square.** Richard immediately recognised it as the one left in his office a few days before. "Open it." Arif demanded.

"I am not in the habit of opening other people's mail."

"I said open it." Richard reluctantly did as he was told, carefully pulled at the rim before removing the large white documents contained inside; the transit certificates were all completed, confirming a shipment of prestigious artefacts to be shipped across the Atlantic to America.

"How did you get these?" Richard asked.

"Don't worry, I'm sure your insurance will cover any damages; we were in and out very quickly and were very discreet, something I know you would appreciate." Richard was still very groggy from the drug and unsure of his surroundings, wondering if he was part of a sick prank.

"Ok I give up, this is all part of some elaborate joke isn't it? Don't tell me, Charlotte's going to jump out any minute ... joke's over you win, I've been severely reprimanded. Now call it off, the joke's gone far enough."

Cassell suddenly punched Richard hard in the chest. "Does that feel like, a joke Richard? Now, tell me what you know, and what you've told the police."

"I have no idea what you're talking about, what police?"

"Southern was in your offices for over an hour on Monday morning, we found these documents, that belong to me, in your safe and you want me to believe you don't know anything? Do you take me for a fool

Richard?" Cassell hit Richard again, punching him in the face.

"I'm telling you I don't know what the fuck you're talking about. I never saw Jonathan. He was supposed to meet me in my offices on Thursday and never showed up. He left that envelope by mistake! It was a mistake, that's all. We put it in the safe expecting him to come and collect it, that's all I know."

"Then you haven't spoken to the Police?"

"No ... no I haven't spoken to anyone ... please I have no idea what any of this is about." As the drug wore off Richard realised this was no joke.

"I want to believe you Richard, I really do, but you see I need to be sure that you're not lying to me. This is a very important shipment and I cannot afford for anything to go wrong. I have to hand it to you Richard, you really are an outstanding character. Early morning jogs, attendances at court, business meetings and of course the lovely Miss Hemmings. So, how does someone like me, get someone like you, with all your standing, all that credibility, to be honest with me to tell me the truth? Can you think of anything Richard? What springs to mind? Is there anything you can think of ... something maybe that reveals a darker side to your character?" The blood appeared to drain from Richard's face.

"Miss Cunningham is a very beautiful woman wouldn't you say?" said Arif with a deadly calm.

"You're bluffing, you wouldn't dare." Richard's heart began to race.

"You disappoint me. I would have thought that you would have known by now that I'm not in the habit of making idle threats." Arif nodded to one of his men who obediently left the room. The room was silent. All that could be heard were the footsteps on the gravel outside, then the creek of what seemed to be a barn door followed by a scurry of further footsteps. Within minutes, the man had returned, accompanied by a very frightened Patsy, gagged with her hands tied behind her back. Hussein remained calm, but Richard, as was so often the case with Patsy, lost all control.

"You bastard I'll kill you!" Richard helplessly tried to struggle free, only to be restrained by Arif's men. Patsy screamed under the gag for him as they tried to reach each other.

"At last, an emotion I understand Richard." said Arif after producing his ace. He waited for Richard's strength to subside. "I have to say, I never thought you had it in you to bag a beauty like this and lawyer to boot, you really have outdone yourself. Tell me is it true what they say about black women in bed? How was she? Was she good? I almost wish I had the time to test out the theory." Arif walked over to Patsy and stroked her face. Patsy pulled away and lashed out with a kick, narrowly missing him. She was quickly restrained. "She has spirit!"

"Take your hands off her," said Richard slowly.

"Arif we have no time for games." said Hussein.

"Now I'll ask you again, tell me what you know."

"Listen I swear to you, I don't know anything."

"Kill her." Richard looked on helplessly as one Arif's men held the knife against Patsy's throat and pulled her head back. Patsy screamed under the gag.

"Please, please." Richard shouted "Don't ... don't hurt her, she's got nothing to do with this! Do what you want with me, but I'm begging you, don't hurt her. I swear to you it's like I said, Jonathan left it in our office, we thought it was a mistake, we tried calling him but he never came back, so we locked it in the safe ... I haven't spoken to anyone about them ... not the police ... not anyone. For Christ's sake! I'm telling you the truth. If I had called the police don't you think they'd be here now! You've got to believe me ... please." The knife now cut into Patsy's skin with Arif's man waiting for the signal to finish what he had started.

"You know something Richard ... I actually believe you. You've convinced me ... but I still have this nagging voice in the back of mind, telling me not to trust you. But I'm a reasonable man, so I've decided to accept your offer. Your life for hers. Cassell you know what to do."

"What about the girl?" Cassell was calm unflinching as he looked at Patsy.

"No I want her alive; I've got plans for Miss Cunningham. Here are your papers Hussein." Arif threw the envelope in Hussein's direction, who began reading through the documents. "I think we can say the shipment is safe…" Arif then turned to Richard shaking his head. "I am sorry Richard, but you see, I can't afford any loose ends, you understand I have no choice in the matter."

One of Arif's men took out a small pistol and held it against Richard's head. Richard said nothing, he only gave Patsy that familiar stare. She screamed, begging them to stop; her voice muffled behind the gag, Richard then closed his eyes, waiting for the click of the trigger.

"Wait," said Hussein "something's missing."

"What are you talking about?" said Arif.

Hussein continued searching through the documents.

"Where's the itinerary?" Hussein asked.

"Don't play games Hussein, each certificate contains details of every item being shipped." Arif grabbed the documents.

"For a shipment this big, the certificates have to be accompanied with an itinerary which must include a full list of the merchandise and its relevant batch number."

"He's right," said Richard, sweating profusely as the gun was still pointed at his head "The shipment won't get through without it, if they don't have it customs will have to go through each batched item individually, which could draw suspicion."

"So why didn't you prepare one!" shouted Arif.

"I'm a courier not a secretary and you said you had this all in hand. Maybe you shouldn't have been so hasty in disposing of your legal adviser." replied Hussein calmly.

Arif started shouting at his men in Arabic. Cassell rushed to the table, looking for additional documents. Richard waited patiently as Cassell turned to Arif, he too addressing him in their mother tongue and, by Arif's raised response, it was clear that he was becoming increasingly frustrated. Throughout, Richard and Hussein remained composed.

"It appears that we do not have this itinerary," Arif tried to conceal his embarrassment.

"Then we have to put one together" said Hussein.

"How long will that take?"

"An hour, maybe more" said Hussein.

"I could do it." said Richard, the gun still levelled at his head.

"Do you take me for a fool Richard?"

"I don't take you for anything. I could use one of your men but the girl would be faster. I need to place the documents in chronological order to make sure they match up with the batch numbers then draft the itinerary in accordance with that. I mean you could take the chance and let them go without it, but as this shipment is obviously so important to you are you prepared to take that chance?" Richard said, legal head screwed firmly on.

"Either you are very clever or very, very stupid." Arif walked back to the window, considering his options. Richard and Hussein avoided each other's gaze, waiting for his decision.

"Untie the girl and I warn you, if you try anything, she will be the first to die." The men untied Patsy and removed the gag, which allowed her to breathe freely. She took a deep breath and was pushed over to a seat in front of Richard. They stared at each other from across the table. Richard managed to give Patsy a secreted smile as the gun was removed from his head. He then passed her a large batch of certificates and asked Arif for some clean sheets of papers on which to prepare the itinerary.

"Patsy each of these certificates contains a batch number with the transit date. I need you to go through them, placing them in a chronological order, and then read them out. Can you do that for me?"

"Yes."

"Good girl."

Patsy began to examine each document, carefully placing the certificates in order. It was a task she could do in no time, but she decided to prolong the process. Richard laid out a blank sheet of paper and proficiently began to draft a heading and columns for the document whilst two of Arif's men looked on. Once the papers were collated, Patsy began to read the batch numbers off to Richard who noted each one down meticulously.

They managed the odd glance from time to time, but as they were being so closely watched, made sure that they stuck to the job at hand. Patsy knew instantly that the itinerary was a red herring, as all the information required was contained within each certificate, but Arif was not as smart as he thought. Richard, and for some reason Hussein, took a chance that paid off and bought him additional time.

* * *

When I said I was on borrowed time, this was not exactly what I had in mind. Arif was clearly a mad man, who had no value for life and took pleasure in bending others to his will, but that was not enough for him; he also revelled in destroying people just for the pleasure of it. As I watched Richard sign our lives away, I couldn't help thinking that had this happened a week before, it would have been Charlotte here instead of me. It would be her watching the last minutes of her life tick away. I had convinced myself that all Richard and I could ever be was a fling; a stab at a moment's happiness, but the last week had carved a bond between us that pushed us both into a direction we really didn't want to go, which eventually led us to this. I knew now that I loved Richard. I suppose I loved him from the instant I first saw him; his sexy features, gentleness and manner made it impossible for me not to fall into the same trap I'm sure so many other women had before me. Love is a gift. I must never forget that and when everything is about to end, love is the only comfort I have left. Yet, something kept telling me to stay strong, not give that sadistic animal the satisfaction of panic because if there was the slimmest chance that Richard had a plan to get us out of here, I must be ready.

* * *

Chapter 27

🜨

Hussein and Arif oversaw the men as they packed the five busts containing the diamonds onto the loaded truck. Hussein had orders to deliver the goods to the docks for transportation and could not afford any slip-ups. He had not accounted for Richard or Patsy. They were a complication that he could have done without. He checked that the lorry seals were in place, but before returning to the farmhouse for the final time, he had to find a way to make one last call.

* * *

Arif had left to check on his precious cargo, leaving me and Richard with two men. One stood by the window with a large gun strapped across his shoulder, whilst the other leaned against the door. They had no clue what we were doing and would have definitely killed us if they had. A small gas lamp flickered on the table, which allowed us to see. Arif made it clear he wanted as little light as possible to ensure no one would be alerted to our presence.

Richard must have fallen foul of his nerves, because he dropped some papers under the table. He asked permission to pick them up and the man by the window nodded, scrutinising Richard's every move as he bent down slowly to retrieve them and return them to their rightful place. He once again gave me a quick glance. He held one of the papers up towards the light inspecting it, but I noticed his focus was elsewhere, it was as if he were photographing parts of the room, noting every minor detail. I summoned up the courage to do the same, making sure I only took fleeting glances, not allowing my gaze to linger. I noticed another small lamp by the window, which stood next to a torn and shabby curtain. There were also newspapers scattered across the room and I could hear the drip of the old rusty tap. I did not know why this was important, but the one thing you learn in law is everything is significant, with the smallest detail sometimes being the make or break of your case. There was a loud crash followed by raised voices. I heard the bleep of a text message, and the man called Cassell removed the phone, and read the message.

"Watch them" ordered Cassell as he left the three of us alone in the room.

On the outside, I was calm, but on the inside I was a quivering wreck with my stomach doing fifty somersaults a second. I had never even seen a real gun before, much less had one pointed at me. I wondered what kind of men it would take to do something like this, but analysing these sub-humans was a fruitless exercise, as I knew no powers of persuasion could be applied to Neanderthals. I was in this stale, dusty room with a man who could, at any moment, end my life; who this time yesterday I didn't even know existed. It was surreal. I kept thinking it was a bad dream and I would eventually wake up. This was no dream. It was real. I was so frightened I could hear my heart beating. I had done nothing wrong and these men had no right to take my future away from me.

Richard took the final sheet from me and brushed his hand against mine. Then, without warning, he broke the rules, rising to his feet, holding the papers and walked towards the man who instinctively aimed the gun in Richard's direction.

"Sit down!" He shouted.

"I just need to go through these with Arif, make sure everything is in order."

"Sit down now!" the man shouted again with his hand on the trigger. I wanted to scream at Richard to do as the gunman asked, but held my tongue.

"Alright, alright calm down, I'm doing as you ask." said Richard as he slowly turned and walked back towards the table. As he was about to sit down, and before I realised what was happening, Richard swiftly grabbed the burning lamp and hurled it across the room, screaming at me to get down. I immediately threw myself under the table as a mass of flames engulfed the window and a spray of gunshots sounded around me. I thought, *that's it, I'm dead,* but out of the blue, the cover of the table was gone as it crashed across the room and I saw Richard struggling with the man.

"Get out Patsy!" screamed Richard as I saw the trap door directly beneath me. The fire, being fuelled by the other lamp and papers, had taken hold while Richard frantically struggled with the man as they rolled around the dusty floor exchanging punches.

"Get out Patsy!" Richard cried again. I used all my strength to pull at the heavy trap door leading to the darkness below. I looked up to a now helpless Richard pinned to the floor, watching in horror as the man had Richard by the throat, squeezing the life out of him. Without thinking, I grabbed the chair, hitting the man across the back of the head; the man collapsed in the room, now filled with smoke.

"Richard please, we have to get out!" my eyes were dripping and Richard began to lift himself up. We both staggered towards our exit, guiding each other into the cellar below.

Richard pulled the trap door shut. "Quick, find something to wedge it with." I disappeared to the end of the stairs, still coughing heavily. I did not discriminate,

I just threw everything until I found an old broom which I rushed back to Richard who lodged it against the trap door to buy us some time.

"The fire will keep them busy but we don't have much time, we've got to find a way out." Richard coughed. I was in shock, functioning on autopilot, doing my best not to think about how we had left the man upstairs. I knew it was him or us, nevertheless I couldn't help feeling like a murderer. Right now, however, all that mattered was finding a way out of this dark hole.

"Look" said Richard, showing me a small ray of moonlight coming from higher up by a wall covered by boxes. Richard pulled at the boxes, which plunged to the floor, revealing a small window that brought some welcome light into the unfamiliar surroundings.

"Is it big enough?" I asked

"It will have to be," said Richard, "I'll need to get it open." Richard carefully climbed onto the boxes until he reached the window and attempted to force it open but it was jammed shut.

"It's jammed, I need something to break it with."

"Won't they hear you?"

"It's a chance we have to take."

"I'll try and find something."

"Hurry Patsy" said Richard, forcing the window in an attempt to dislodge it.

I scrambled around through the pockets of light, searching for anything that may help us. There was junk everywhere and I felt something furry scuttle across my leg. I squealed in fear, doing all I could to hold myself together. Deep in a corner I saw what I could just make out to be a pile of clothing. I stumbled over the rubbish and clumsily fell onto the large heap. I began slowly crawling over it, feeling my way as I went. Suddenly I came to the realisation that it was not a pile of clothes at all but a body. I screamed at the top of lungs.

"What is it?" said Richard losing his footing as he crashed to the floor.

"There's someone down here!"

"Where?"

"Over there in that corner. I thought it was a pile of clothes but it feels like a body!" I whimper as Richard held me.

"Wait here" he said but I was shaking all over and had no intention of letting him go so I held tightly onto the tail of his jacket as he made his way into the crevice of darkness in the corner of the room, only releasing him as he bent down to find out what it was I had found. Richard felt his way around the thing, gradually working his way up until he found the cold exterior of a face. He jumped back in shock, then returned to examine the body. He cautiously turned the face towards the light only to discover that it was Jonathan Southern's dead eyes staring back at him.

"Is he…" I asked

"Yes"

"Oh my God, are you sure?"

"I'm sure."

Then suddenly as I watched Richard gently close the empty, lifeless eyes, I was catapulted back to twelve years before; to a musty, cold room with boarded windows; where a terrified sixteen-year-old girl spent five endless days of her life. I never really noticed Samuel Meadows; he worked around the School, doing as he was told and like most people, I never paid him much attention. Anyway, back then, I had far more important things on my mind, such as finding ways to survive from one day to next. To the world, I was bright, accomplished Patsy Cunningham earning a scholarship to the prestigious St Ignatius Grammar School for Girls. Yet, for four years of my life, I suffered relentless verbal and physical abuse at the hands of my peers, too cowardly, too afraid to speak out. They were led by the General, Cynthia Bradley; a stream of destructive energy, who was the most popular, and by far the most beautiful girl in school. She was also a master of manipulation. Tormenters come in all shapes and sizes but the one common denominator between them is the need to possess power. They search for a victim, someone who is different in some way.

I was perfect; the only black girl in the school, whose parents were not rich and lived in a small terraced house on the poorer side of the Town. It didn't help that I always came top in my class, winning awards of excellence every year, which placed Cynthia in second place, somewhere she hated to be.

Cynthia methodically and ruthlessly broke me down, and with every tear she and her pack invoked, every fearful moment they created, their power grew stronger. I became so weak that I even started to see myself that way; conditioned into believing I was worthless, useless. All I had was my books, my studies, and as a young girl, it filled every waking day. I cut myself off from everyone and it was only by immense persistence on Anna's part that she became my only friend.

Yet, the truth has a way of revealing itself; and by a twist of fate, a teacher got hold of footage of my abuse on a mobile phone; and just like that, Cynthia Bradley's reign of terror was over. Of course, no one believed that this clean cut and cultured girl could ever have been a part of this; so my peers blamed me for Cynthia's downfall. But none of us realised that Samuel Meadows loathed me most of all. He despised me for taking away the only thing he ever truly loved: Cynthia Bradley. Samuel had convinced himself that he and Cynthia had a bond that no-one could break, he created a shrine of her; through hundreds of pictures and pages of diaries of Cynthia's comings and goings. Therefore, it was not surprising that when Samuel took his obsession one-step further and kidnapped Cynthia, that he took me too; holding us prisoners in separate rooms. She was the love of his life; and I was paraded as his trophy, his way of proving how far he was prepared to go to show just how much he loved her.

Cynthia was a master of persuasion and she used her time well, convincing Samuel that she would run away with him; if he did one thing – kill me. I can still see the glimmer of that knife now, raised above my head, waiting for the darkness of death, and Cynthia's words are as clear now as they were then: *"No let me do it."* Cynthia's voice was calm, and I really believed she meant to kill me that day. I truly believed she hated me that much; then the knife fell...

"Patsy! Patsy!" Richard was rigorously shaking me, propelling me back into the uncomfortable reality of the smoke-filled room. I was sobbing uncontrollably and could not stop. "I understand ... I know what happened to you." I told Richard everything, released the trauma of twelve years before without even realising I was doing it.

"I'm sorry ... I can't go through this again Richard ... I can't ... don't you see, I'm back where I started ... back in that room, but this time there's no way out. That man, he's dead, he's dead Richard ... just like Samuel Meadows ... those empty cold eyes."

"I know ... but we're alive Patsy ... we are alive." Richard continued to shake me. I screamed into his arms, squeezing him hard, not wanting to let go and praying that I would wake up from this terrible nightmare.

"Richard I don't understand! None of this makes any sense." The smoke now filled the cellar and we were finding it hard to breath. Richard grabbed my face.

"Listen we can get out of here, we can make it."

"But…"

"No buts, if you don't come with me we'll die here together because I won't go without you. Patsy … Patsy … listen to me. Do you really think I could spend another second in this world without you in it? We've shared more in the last few days than people who have a life time together; we can't let that end here, there is so much more for us, so much more. Now we have a fighting chance if we leave, but none if we stay."

I wasn't sure if Richard, like Cynthia, was doing what he did best, using his amazing powers of persuasion to get what he wanted, or if he truly and actually loved me, but whether his words were said in truth or not, they had the desired effect because I realised that I wanted a fighting chance to be with him and live. His gentle kiss to my forehead acted like a sedative, seeping its way through my body, calming me down and through the murky air, we kissed. He then took my hand and led me back towards the waiting window and our only way out.

Chapter 28

❦

Arif and his men looked on helplessly as the farmhouse burned crackling, lighting up the night sky.

"What about Ali?" asked Cassell.

"He was a fool, let him burn," replied Arif coldly. "And you're lucky I don't throw you in there with him."

"But I heard the crash and shouting and thought you needed me."

"For what, for this?" Arif slapped Cassell hard in the face as the other men watched, stone faced.

"I'm sorry but…"

"But what?" screamed Arif

"They're pen pushers! I never expected…" Arif grabbed Cassell hard by the throat, squeezing tightly and Cassell fought for breath.

"You better start praying Cassell, because if you've let them get away and I don't find those documents I will kill you myself, do you hear me?" said Arif with a threatening whisper before throwing him to the floor. "Now all of you circle around the back. If I know

Templeton, he found a way out. Move! This fire will bring everyone down on us."

* * *

Richard pushed and prodded as we both used all our strength to lever me out of the small window and, even though the air was thick with the smell of smoke, the freshness of the outside brought welcome relief. I scrambled and scratched my way out, but kept slipping back. I fought hard, grappling and clutching anything I could find, finally grasping a small branch, which allowed me to steady myself before I made another attempt. I could hear Richard coughing heavily beneath me and knew that if I did not make it now, we would both perish. My hands slipped on the soft dirt as I kept hold of the fragile branch. Richard was really struggling so I scraped at the window, trying to dig my fingers into the earth, making every attempt to get more leverage. It was no use. I felt my body sliding back and the branch begin to give way. I watched helplessly as it started cracking, one piece at a time, spelling the end for both of us. As it snapped and my hand fell away, someone grabbed me.

"Don't be frightened. I'm here to help you" said Hussein as he pulled me through the window.

* * *

I shivered in the cold as Hussein kicked the window from the outside and carefully lowered both hands inside.

"Quickly take my hand" Hussein told Richard, who was waiting below. I wanted to help but knew I would only get in the way. Instead, I kept watch as I could hear Arif's men close by. Hussein struggled as he lifted Richard up towards the small opening but he was strong and managed to get Richard far enough, which allowed Richard to manoeuvre himself into a position that enabled him to pull his way through. Once out, Richard lay coughing uncontrollably, gasping for breath, before finally scrambling to his feet. I rushed into his arms, relieved that we were out and together. Richard held me and stared at Hussein with suspicion.

"We don't have much time, Arif's men will be here any minute" said Hussein.

"Why should we trust you?" said Richard as he removed his jacket and wrapped it around me, bringing me comfort in the cold dark night.

"Because right now, Templeton, I'm your only hope. I'll explain everything later but now we have to go. Do you know how to use one of these?" Hussein pulled a gun from his inside pocket and passed it to Richard who examined it.

"No but I'm a fast learner."

"Why doesn't that surprise me?" replied Hussein "Come on and stay close."

Richard held the gun in one hand and mine in the other and I was disgusted with myself because at a time that I should be quaking with fear, not knowing whether I would live or die, all I could think about was how sexy Richard looked with his gun and loosened tie. He was truly my own James Bond. However, the fantasy didn't last long as Arif's men seemed to be getting closer and closer, snapping me quickly back into reality.

Hussein peered around the corner of the house and turned to us whispering, "We need to get to that" pointing to a large lorry in the front of the muddy driveway.

"We'll never make it in that," replied Richard.

"Listen I've been tracking those diamonds for the last two years and I have no intention of leaving without them. You can always go it alone Templeton, but you know as well as I do that we stand a better chance if we stick together." I squeezed Richard's arm making my feelings clear that I wanted us to stay with Hussein because, even though I trusted Richard, Hussein seemed to know what he was doing and we needed each other. Richard reluctantly nodded in agreement.

A man was standing by the lorry with a large rifle strapped across his chest.

"Stay here," Hussein crouched on all fours as he crawled across the cold dirt. He was amazing, expertly plotting his way whilst securing his invisibility. He covered so much ground so quickly, getting within spitting distance of the man within minutes. Then he waited patiently for the right moment and, as if on cue, the sentry took his hand off his rifle to light a cigarette and, without warning, Hussein jumped him, hitting him hard on the back of the head with his pistol. The man was knocked out instantly. Hussein beckoned us over with a frantic wave of his arms. Richard grabbed my hand, telling me to stay down while Hussein loosened the rifle and he and Richard pulled the unconscious man behind some nearby bushes.

The lorry was enormous and it seemed a million miles to the large cab, but before I knew what was happening, Richard was pushing me into it as he and Hussein got in on either side. Hussein fiddled around for the keys, lodged deep in his jacket pocket.

"It's very accommodating of Arif to leave those with you," said Richard.

"Let's just say I have friends in high places ... Get down. All hell is going to break loose when I start this baby." Richard buried my head in his arms, covering me with his body. I started to pray as I clung onto him. Hussein turned the key in the ignition that released the roar of the engine, immediately alerting Arif and his men.

"Stop them!" Arif screamed as Hussein rammed his foot hard on the pedal. There was a flurry of bullets causing the windows of the cab to crash around us. Richard shielded me as we crouched down as far as we could. The lorry collided with something I couldn't see, but whatever it was sent a barrage of metal into every direction. I felt Richard flinch and tried to get up but he held me firmly, preventing me from moving. Splinters of glass were everywhere and Richard's arm felt wet. I knew something was wrong and pulled at him to let me up.

"Keep her down." Hussein shouted, but I had had enough of taking orders and pushed Richard off me only to find his right arm covered in blood.

"Richard you're hurt!" I screamed.

"Get down" Richard replied as he clutched at his arm.

"No!" I yelled at him, ducking under the bullets that were now coming from behind us. I desperately searched around the disorganised cab for something, anything to help stop the bleeding.

"My inside pocket" said Richard in pain. I hunted around in Richard's pockets and found a large handkerchief, which I hastily pulled out, but to my surprise the transfer certificates fell out with it.

"Insurance" said Richard and I was careful to put the certificates back where I found them. I was at a loss as to what to do, there was a large piece of glass lodged in Richard's arm.

"What do I do? I don't know what to do..." I shout.

Hussein was quick to respond. "Don't try to remove it, if you do, you're going to cause more harm. You need to control the bleeding, carefully wrap the handkerchief around the wound ... try to stop the glass from moving ... careful ... don't press too hard." There was no time to think as I followed Hussein's instructions. Richard bit his lower lip but did not make a sound as I covered the wound.

"Is it bad?" asked Hussein.

"I'll live" replied Richard as he leaned back while I continued to secure the handkerchief.

"The worst of it is behind us now."

"But won't they come after us?" Hussein's silence told me all I needed to know. I brushed Richard's forehead, now soaked in sweat, and Hussein remained focused on the road as the large headlamps led the way.

"How's he holding up?" asked Hussein.

"He needs a doctor." I said as the blood began to seep through the impromptu bandage.

"Arif's men won't be far away, we need to keep moving." said Hussein with one eye on the road and the other on his side view mirrors.

"Why are you helping us?" I asked Hussein, taking off the jacket and wrapping it around Richard who was beginning to shiver.

"I've been working undercover for the American Government."

"This just gets better and better." Richard murmured.

"Two years ago, diamonds valued at thirty million pounds were stolen from a train en route to the Bank of

England. They caught the gang responsible but never found the diamonds" said Hussein.

"And Arif?"

"He financed it and was responsible for moving the diamonds out of the country, but we had no proof and just as we were getting close, we received a mysterious tip regarding the gangs' whereabouts. Before any pay-out could be made linking him to the raid or any of the men could be brought to trial, they all met with unfortunate accidents in prison.

"You think Arif was behind it?" I asked beginning to piece the segments together for the first time.

"It would be too coincidental for him not to have been. Picture it, no one left to implicate him, no pay-outs and the icing on the cake, he gets to keep the lot. We've been hitting dead ends for nearly a year and then, a few months ago, I received a tip that someone was trying to buy their way into one of the biggest crime syndicates on the West Coast, and they were using over twenty million dollars' worth of diamonds to do it." Hussein looked hard in his rear mirror at the headlights in the distance. "The syndicate Arif is trying to join are big players. It's not just about the money; you also have to come with connections. They have congressmen and even senators on their payroll. Arif had to show he had the right people in his pocket, people with money, reputation and influence. Harvey was able to introduce him to those people. Here they come, hold on!" Hussein pushed down hard on the pedal, peering at the headlights coming towards us.

I could see two, no, three large Range Rovers in the side mirrors, one managed to get along side of us, his horn blaring and headlights flashing. Hussein swerved into the Rover which, of course, was much quicker and more nimble than we were. I noticed another large Rover on the other side of us but the road was so narrow the driver screeched at his brakes to prevent it from colliding with us. Arif's men were determined and it seemed nothing could stop them.

"They are trying to run us off the road!" Shouted Hussein, finding it hard to control the steering wheel as one of the Rovers smashed into our side. I held tightly onto Richard, whose arm was still bleeding heavily. One of the Rovers then managed to squeeze its way in front of us while the other replaced it along our side, boxing us in, leaving nowhere to go. Hussein jammed his foot onto the accelerator, ramming the Rover in front, but it did not have the desired effect as the Rover was sturdy and simply kept on going. Both Rovers on either side began veering into us, sending us in all directions. There was hardly any space, but the Rovers stuck to us like glue.

"Alright I've had enough of this" said Hussein and sharply turned the steering wheel smashing into one of the Rovers, sending it crashing into the grass verge and hurtling into the air, falling heavily back onto the road behind us whilst rolling over and over again before the smashed up vehicle landed on its roof.

"One down, two to go" said Hussein, remaining amazingly composed. Our victory, however, was short lived as the roof of the Rover in front opened up and a man stood up pointing what looked like a machine gun directly at us.

"Get down!" Hussein yelled as the sea of bullets came towards us. I held Richard down and we crouched as far as we could but nothing could protect us from the onslaught.

"I'm losing control!" screamed Hussein as some of the bullets ricocheted off the cab window whilst others penetrated through, sending the lorry into a massive skid and, despite Hussein's gallant efforts, careening down a steep verge. Hussein held on, placing all his pressure onto the brakes in the hope that we could stay in one piece. "We're not going to make it!" Hussein cried and I prayed for another miracle but realised that nothing could help us now. Then everything went black.

Chapter 29

I do not know how long I was out but the cold air told me that I was no longer in the cab. Either I'd been pulled free or was thrown clear, I didn't know which. My head throbbed and I found it difficult to open my eyes. I raised my hand to my forehead and a trickle of blood ran down my face. I slowly lifted myself up, holding my head in agony, but as far as I could tell that was my only injury. I opened my eyes, trying to work out what had happened. Then it hit me, I was alone; Richard and Hussein were nowhere to be seen. I felt dizzy and found it hard to stand. I was staggering and unsteady on my feet but I knew I had to move as quickly as possible because I had no idea where Arif's men were. I heard shouting in the distance and saw the lorry wedged up against a tree and I stumbled over to look inside, frightened of what I would find. I awkwardly climbed up and was relieved to find the cab empty, Richard's jacket lay on the cab floor and there were traces of blood on the seat. I quickly grabbed the jacket and put it on, there was a rustling noise in the bushes behind me. I froze, frightened to breath.

"They have to be here somewhere, keep looking" I recognised Arif's voice and asked God's forgiveness as I was hoping he had been in the vehicle that Hussein annihilated earlier. I found the courage to lower myself back down onto the ground and could hear his men getting closer. I had no idea what to do and wished Richard was with me. I thought of running to the cover of the thick bushes behind me but it would be impossible to make it. Suddenly someone covered my mouth and bundled me away from the cab.

Hussein threw me hard into the dirt, lying on top of me still covering my mouth. I could hear footsteps all around us cracking and snapping the crisp leaves as we lay motionless. Usually I hated the dark, but now was grateful for its protection.

"Can it be moved?" I heard Arif ask.

"We'll have to winch it up" one of the men replied as we heard the lorry start up.

"Then do it, we've lost enough time!" shouted Arif in frustration. The men started shouting at each other in their mother tongue. There seemed to be confusion about how best to carry out Arif's orders. After a while, it appeared a consensus was reached as I could hear some of them scuttling back up the verge. There was a deadly silence that I did not understand. I tried to move but Hussein pinned me down. There was a mist in the air, an uneasy quiet that both of us could feel. It was then that I felt the cold steel of a gun against the back of head.

"Well, well, well, look what we have here," said Arif.

* * *

"Stop it you'll kill him." I screamed as Arif's men continued to punch Hussein repeatedly, kicking him in the chest and stomach as he coughed uncontrollably in the dirt. I watched as a man pulled him up by the hair, slapping him across the face. The lorry was being winched back to the main road with the help of the remaining two large land rovers and the roar of the engines were deafening.

"Please stop, you're killing him." I begged but the onslaught continued with the men striking at every part of Hussein's body until he was close to unconsciousness.

"That's enough." Arif finally said. The men picked up Hussein, dragging him over to the tree and propping him up as his head flopped in front of him. One man pulled him up by his hair so that Arif could stare him in the eye.

"Who are you?" said Arif menacingly, leaning in close and whispering into Hussein's ear. I was amazed at Hussein's resilience as he just smiled and said nothing.

Arif walked away as if pondering what to do. I looked over at Hussein, tears in my eyes, wanting to suffer for him and knowing that, had it not been for us, he would have got away. I didn't even know if there was an us anymore. Richard had disappeared and for all I knew he was lying dead somewhere, alone and in the dark. Then Arif turned his attentions to me, summoning his men to bring me over. I knew he and his men were sadistic bastards, so prepared myself for the worst. As he gently stroked my face, I tried to pull away because even the thought of his hands on me made my skin crawl.

"You've had quite an eventful week Miss Cunningham, and all for a man who appears to have deserted you in favour of saving his own skin. Tell me, where's Templeton?"

"I don't know." I said, trying my best to hold it together. Arif then grabbed the lapel of the jacket, dragging me towards him so that I could smell his breath.

"I said, where is he?" he screamed.

"I don't know! And even if I did, I'd never tell you. You sadistic creep." I could not understand where this courage was coming from, but as far as I was concerned I was dead anyway so why give him the satisfaction of fear? Nothing comes for free and Arif made me pay for that statement with a stinging slap across my face, leaving me dazed.

"Take pleasure in beating on women Arif?" said Hussein, weak from his own beating.

"I take pleasure in everything I do." Arif showed no remorse for his actions, slapping me again, this time knocking me to the floor and causing the papers in the inside pocket to become dislodged.

"Arif bent down removing the papers from their hiding place. "You really are full of surprises."

"And you're full of shit." I responded with hatred burning through me. Arif laughed out loud, pointing at me and turning to his men, saying something that once again, I could not understand. They responded with sniggers, making it clear to me that the joke was at my expense, suddenly taking me back to that young girl I had once been, surrounded by a pack of bullies. Arif slowly removed his jacket and passed it to one of his men.

"Do you know what makes the world go around Patsy?" asked Arif as he approached me "Power and control." He continued walking towards me and I instinctively started to back away. "And right now I have all the power, the control and that gives me the right to take what I want." My heart was beating so hard it almost leapt out of my chest, because I knew where this was going.

"I'll die before I let you touch me." I whispered as the tears streamed down my face.

"Oh you'll die alright, but only after I've finished with you." Arif yanked me towards him, grabbing me tightly around the waist as his men looked on. I felt his hands crawling their way up my skirt and his wet and slimy tongue licked my neck and face. No woman prepares herself for something like this; what do you do? This animal was pawing at me, trying to destroy me by forcing himself on me. I could feel his hands groping every part of my body, squeezing my buttocks, gripping my breasts so ferociously that I arched in pain. The laughter grew louder until it was all around me; Hussein struggled in his weakened state to help me, but it was in vain. I felt Arif's hands push their way between my legs attempting to force them apart. Sometimes self-preservation isn't all there is. I had spent the last few days of my life in a sort of trance with a man who I had come to love; who had opened me up to experiences most people could only dream of and I could not let my last memory on this earth be something crude and violent. I had to dig deeper in myself than ever before. I knew what the outcome would be, but I could not just allow this to happen to me. As Arif attempted to lower me to the musty ground, his hands still tugging at my panties, I took every ounce of strength I had left, biting hard on his face, tearing away at his flesh with my teeth and not letting go until I tasted his blood in my mouth. Arif screeched in pain he pulled away, giving me the opportunity to pull my legs free and kicking him so hard in the ribs that I felt my bone buckle. It had the desired effect, it got him off me as he collapsed in agony, screaming and cursing. I tried to run, but was held tight by his men who forced both my arms behind my back, making me wait for their boss to inflict the inevitable retribution.

It took a long time for Arif's pain to subside and I smugly grinned as he rolled around suffering, still cursing as he finally struggled to his feet.

"You fucking bitch!" he said still holding his bleeding face, breathing heavily and it gave me great pleasure to respond to his comment with a defiant smile. It did not matter now because even if he wanted to, he was in too much pain to finish the job. I did not think I had the capacity to hate someone so much and in all honesty, if I'd had a knife in my hand I would have happily gutted him like a fish without a second thought. I suppose it's true when they say that violence begets violence. I didn't feel fear, I was too angry for that and if the end meant this creep would never lay those filthy hands on me again, it would be a welcome relief. Arif grabbed the small pistol from one of his men, smiling as he pointed it at my head and began to squeeze the trigger. I looked over at Hussein and smiled and then in a flash, a sudden bang sent the gun flying from Arif's hand. I could see Arif's blood and realised that the power of the bullet had literally sent the gun ricocheting away.

I could not believe my eyes as I saw a disorientated Richard pointing a gun at Arif, his arm covered in blood, with the blooded handkerchief still in place.

Richard was finding it hard to stop the gun from shaking but he kept it aimed at his target.

"Patsy, over here now!" said Richard as the sweat poured down his forehead, there was a large tear in his trousers and a deep gash across his leg which could only have been caused by the accident. It was clear Richard was finding it hard to focus his vision.

"Patsy!" I ran over to him, instinctively standing behind him.

"Tell your men to throw their weapons over here Arif ... Now!" Arif held his arm wincing in pain as he swayed from side to side.

"You really do have nine lives Richard, but the cards are stacked against you. You can hardly stand. How long do you think it will be before my men will finish you?"

"Not before I got to you first and, like most cowards, I don't think you're ready to die just yet" Richard pulled the safety on the gun back with great difficulty. Arif, being the coward he was, slowly nodded to his men to discard their weapons.

"Hussein ... Hussein" Richard called "Are you still with us?"

"Just about" Hussein replied weakly.

"Let him go." Richard demanded and Arif nodded to his men to do as they were told. Hussein fell to the floor as the men released him, but found the strength to pick himself up and make his way over to Richard and me.

There I was in the middle of this standoff with two men who were close to death's door and all these other men around us just waiting for the opportunity to jump Richard and disarm him.

At first I thought the sounds of the police sirens were just my imagination, but realised this was not the case as I could hear them getting closer and closer. I heard cars above us screeching to a halt and those beautiful blue lights were flashing above us. Even though Hussein was in pain, he summoned up the energy to scramble to his feet.

"Do you hear that Arif? That sound signifies you're finished, over" said Hussein.

"But how could you…"

"You said it yourself, everyone has a price and the higher the stakes the further they're prepared to go. Isn't that right Cassell?" Hussein turned to Cassell. "Who do you think planted the tracking device that brought them here?"

Arif shook with anger disbelieving that he had been so careful, planning everything so well, only to be betrayed by one of his own. Cassell didn't bother to deny it; things had gone too far for that.

"Why?" Arif asked, bewildered.

"Spare me your hurt Arif, I've been with you since the beginning, when you were less than nothing. I was the only true and loyal friend you had."

"You betray me and you talk about loyalty!"

"I do talk about it because it's a word that you don't understand! My brother trusted you! He came to you with a plan and you used him then had him killed. What, you think I didn't know? That I'm that naïve that dense that I couldn't figure it out? Yes I betrayed you and I'd do it again."

"Your life is over Cassell. You think they can protect you? Where do you think a traitor like you can go?"

"With you, straight to hell" said Cassell as he lunged at Arif. They fell in each other's grips as police began to scramble down the steep verge and a large police helicopter thundered, almost blinding us with its beaming light turning the dirt into gusts of dusty smoke around us.

"This is the Police, don't move; stay where you are!" The sound was deafening but nothing could deter the violence that had erupted between Arif and Cassell. Arif's men, knowing there was no way out, scattered, disappearing into the brush. The sheer force of the helicopter above made us all unsteady on our feet and Richard, already weak, struggled to stay upright. I held onto him but knew he could not stay conscious for much longer and prayed that the police would reach us in time. Cassell managed to get Arif into a headlock and, with his arms firmly in place, used all his strength to squeeze the life out of the struggling Arif.

"No Cassell, we need him alive," shouted Hussein who tried, unsuccessfully, to rise to his feet.

"I'm done with making deals" said Cassell, only tightening his grip around Arif's throat. Any other man would have submitted, but not Arif. I watched as he grabbed hard on Cassell's testicles, causing him to screech in pain as he is hurtled back into a tree behind him. Cassell crashed to the ground, giving Arif the upper hand. We all looked on in horror as Arif wasted no time picking up a heavy rock and smashing Cassell repeatedly until the rock was covered in blood and Cassell lay motionless on the ground, his head caved in.

"That's what you get for betraying me." Arif remorselessly spat on Cassell, whose blank eyes were open, lifeless. I had never been so scared of another human being in my life. Arif was consumed with hate, taking pleasure in this hideous act of violence, with his bloodied face and murderous hands, looking like a wild animal. As the police made their way down, he knew there was no way out. He turned towards us in a last hope to escape, staring at Richard who held the gun firmly in his hands, but as Arif walked slowly towards him, he couldn't pull the trigger. No matter what he had just witnessed, Richard could not kill a man, not even a man like Arif.

"Shoot!" screamed Hussein, making a hopeless plunge at Arif, which only resulted in him being knocked to the ground and suffering further merciless kicks to his body. Richard finally pulled at the trigger, wounding Arif in the arm, but it was as if he were a man possessed. Before anyone could stop him, he ran at Richard, resulting in them struggling, but Richard was too weak to overcome him and the gun skidded to the floor followed by Richard who now lay face down in the dirt. The lights and piercing roar of the helicopter were still all around us and, as Arif held the heavy rock, still covered in Cassell's blood, as he stood over Richard, I heard him say.

"Time to die," He prepared to crash the bloodied rock into Richard.

Suddenly another gun fired and, as Arif fell to the floor, I heard it thunder again and again until all that was left was the click of an empty chamber. It was only when the police officer took the gun from my hand that I realised the shots had been fired by me.

Chapter 30

Joyce kept vigil over her sister as she slept, smiling at the nurse who checked Patsy's pulse. Their parents were on their way and she didn't have a clue what to tell them. How could she explain Patsy being in the middle of nowhere, having nearly died at the hands of a madman?

"How's she doing?" asked Hussein as he entered, supported by two crutches.

"Five stitches to the head and a mild concussion; they're keeping her sedated." Replied Joyce, not taking her eye off her sister for a moment.

"She's a brave woman."

"What's going to happen to her?" asked Joyce.

"Your sister saved our lives and, once I complete my report, there will be no action taken against her."

"Will she be safe? Won't they come after her?"

"Arif's dead and all his men have been captured and are in custody. The diamonds have been recovered. It's over."

"I blame Templeton for this, if he hadn't gone near Patsy, none of this would have happened."

"Don't be too hard on him."

"He nearly got her killed … how is he anyway?"

"Critical, but the good news is, he's stable."

"Where is he now?"

"He's been moved to one of the private wards on the fifth floor."

"Figures … listen I want Patsy's name kept out of this. If anyone was to find out she was involved in something like this…"

"Don't worry, I'll take care of everything." said Hussein.

"You'd better."

* * *

The bright lights and white walls were a contrast from the dank and dark farmhouse and cellar that had been my prison just hours before, but it was as if my brain was trying to catch up with itself, piecing bits of the night together as if it were a puzzle scattered across a kitchen table. I was so confused, not sure if it had all actually happened; but it must have, I could not have dreamt it.

Joyce lay asleep in the chair next to my bed; she was holding my hand, stirring quietly. I squeezed it and watched as she slowly opened her eyes.

"Hey, how are you feeling?"

"Where am I?" I asked, frightened and unsure of my surroundings. Then it hit me like a bolt and everything suddenly came flooding back. I wasn't spared from one harrowing moment. It was as if the entire night was playing itself back over and over again in slow motion in my head. I began to sob and grabbed my sister, thanking God that I had the comfort of her arms around me, something I thought I would never experience again.

"Joyce ... I killed him ... I had no choice, he was evil Joyce and he tried to ... he tried to ..." Joyce held me tightly, trying to calm me down.

"I know, I know, there was nothing you could do. It's all over now. He can't hurt you anymore ... I'm here and I'm not going anywhere. I'm here."

* * *

I still felt a little dizzy as I made my way through the hospital corridor. It took all my energy to persuade Joyce to get something to eat, but she looked shattered and had not left my side so I was glad that she finally took my advice, which didn't happen that often. It was clear that she was in no mood to discuss Richard. She was still too angry, blaming him for everything that had happened, so I decided to leave the subject alone. I staggered, leaning against the hospital wall for support, steadying myself, heading towards the Agnes Ward where I knew Richard was fighting for his life.

The doctors and nurses hovered around, none of them worrying about me as I continued in my quest to find Richard. Maybe I was just a glutton for punishment, but I felt empty without him and was beside myself with worry, which was not making me any better. As I turned into the ward, my heart skipped a beat at the thought of seeing him again. I hung around outside, trying to summon the courage to go in and finally, after a number of reassuring thoughts convincing myself that everything would be fine, I tentatively made my way through the large double doors.

The reception nurse smiled. "Can I help you?" she said in her pristine white uniform.

"Hi, can you help me, I'm looking for ..." but before I could finish the sentence, a blond woman rushed and pushed past me.

"I'm so sorry" the young woman said, apologising for her rudeness and I nodded, stepping aside as she looked so panicked that I could not help feeling sorry for her.

"Richard ... Richard Templeton, he was brought in seriously hurt in the early hours of this, morning I need to see him."

"And you are?" The nurse asked.

"Charlotte Hemmings, his fiancée." Even in her ruffled and distraught state, Charlotte looked beautifully put together with her long blond hair sitting uncomfortably on the shoulders of her thick fur coat.

She was wearing an elegant evening gown and had limitless class which could have only come with money and breeding. Her pictures did not do her justice, as she was even more beautiful in the flesh with porcelain skin reddened by her haste.

"Charlotte!" A man called from further down the corridor. He was a handsome man with a thick head of light grey hair looking worried in a green jumper and smart black trousers. I knew immediately that it was Richard's father. Even his voice sounded the same. Charlotte ran towards the man and I watched, unobserved as she fell into his arms in complete panic.

"It's alright he's resting and he's stable." I heard the man say as he glanced over at me, I quickly looked away pretending to read some notices on the wall behind me.

"John what happened?" Charlotte asked.

"I'm not sure but the most important thing is that he's safe."

"Can I see him?"

"Of course" I continued to pretend to read but then turned to see Charlotte being taken into a room, her eyes lighting up as she entered, the way mine would have done if it had been me.

Everything I wanted was in that room. The trouble was that it belonged to someone else. It's difficult not to accept your wrongdoing when it is staring you in the face. From the moment, I knew about Charlotte, it was wrong for me to carry on. It made no difference that I had fallen hopelessly in love because you can lie to everyone but not to yourself. The fact was that by being with Richard, I was going against everything I believed in. Maybe seeing Charlotte today and watching the close relationship between her and Richard's father was God's way of telling me that enough is enough. Why did all of this happen to me? I couldn't help thinking that it was some kind of retribution. All my life I'd dreamt of feeling this kind of love, what woman wouldn't? Logically speaking, Richard had his life, and I had mine and even though we couldn't be together it didn't mean that my life would be an empty one. It's only when you have to fight for your life that you begin to understand and appreciate how precious it is. When this happened to me years ago, I thought the way to cope was to cut myself off, not trust anyone, close myself off from the world; but I was wrong. Richard and I needed each other to get through and we did. He saved me and I saved him and thanks to our strength and the help of Hussein we were both still breathing.

As I left the ward, I found Joyce waiting patiently outside. It figured that she would know exactly where I would be, but there was no admonishment, just a strong and silent support. I really loved my sister and was sorry for what I had put her through.

"Let's go home." I said.

"Ok Sis" Joyce replied, helping me back to the ward where my parents were now waiting.

* * *

"Thank God." A distraught Martha Templeton greeted Charlotte, before returning to Richard's bedside where he lay in a coma, she held his hand gently and beckoned Charlotte towards her. "Look Richard … Charlotte's here." Charlotte made her way to the other side of the bed, gently stroking Richard's hand, before kissing him on the forehead, shocked to see his badly beaten body covered in bandages.

"Richard, darling it's me, I'm here. Richard can you hear me? Please talk to me … John, what happened?" Charlotte asked, her gaze fixed on Richard.

"I'm still not sure, the police won't tell us anything, but my only concern right now is Richard."

"Will he be alright?"

"He's injuries are not as bad as they look and he is suffering from severe shock."

"The Police have been asking all kinds of questions about Harvey, but they will not tell us anything."

Richard struggled to find his way out of the dark; he could hear voices but was not sure where they were coming from. He was searching for something precious that he had lost. What was he looking for? Suddenly the shade of night subsided, giving way to a clear new day; he looked up to see a bright sun, piercing through a blue sky. Someone took his hand and when he turned, Patsy was standing by his side. "Where have you been Richard? I've been looking for you everywhere!" said Patsy.

"I've been looking for you too, where did you go?"

"Not far, just over that hill. You should see it Richard, it's beautiful. Come on, we can go there now, together." As Patsy pulled him towards the hill, Richard's feet were fixed to the ground, preventing him from moving, he tried to move but could not. He felt the grip of Patsy's hand loosen as she ran ahead of him.

"Wait Patsy ... Wait I can't keep up."

"Come on Richard, it's just over that hill. It's beautiful! You have to see it." She was running so fast he was beginning to lose sight of her.

"Patsy ... Wait! ... Don't go without me ... Please wait, Patsy ... Patsy!"

"He's coming round ... Charlotte talk to him," John Templeton said watching Richard's every move.

"He's trying to say something. Richard ... Richard ... it's Charlotte. I'm with you my darling and I'm not going anywhere."

Chapter 31

❦

Three months later

Hussein marvelled at the splendour of the banqueting suite situated in the heart of London, surveying the large room of people who looked as if they had enough money to settle the national debt. He had spent most of his adult life living on a wing and prayer, but mingling amongst this decadence made it clear to him that he would not change places with any of them for world. He was on a long leave of absence, under strict orders to rest, recoup. He was finding it hard to assimilate back into normal society after being on the outskirts of it for so long.

"I didn't think you'd make it." Hussein turned to find a fully recovered Richard standing behind him.

"You know me Templeton, never one to turn down a free meal."

"My don't you scrub up well" replied Richard, clocking Hussein's smart black dinner suit as both men shook hands with enthusiasm.

"Well I wouldn't like to bring down the tone of the place, and what a place. I must say Templeton you don't do anything by halves."

"You know me Hussein, I aim to please and am not one to disappoint."

"I'd second that," said Charlotte as she grabbed Richard lovingly by the arm.

"Hussein let me introduce Charlotte Hemmings" said Richard.

"My pleasure" Hussein extended his hand, which Charlotte accepted.

"No the pleasure's all mine and I know that it's mainly thanks to you that he's safe and sound and for that I will be eternally grateful. Promise me you won't leave before we get a chance to get to know each other."

"Now that would be my pleasure." Hussein bent down as he gently kissed Charlotte's hand.

"Charming as well as handsome! Hey Templeton, I hope you've got a fantastic speech prepared." said Charlotte.

"In the bag" replied Richard.

"Oh there's Lizzy, I've got to go over, she's absolutely green with envy" Charlotte expertly manoeuvred her way through the room.

"She's stunning," said Hussein, watching Charlotte as she made pleasant conversation. "How much does she know?"

"Only what she needed to. Thanks for your discretion ... Have you seen her? ... Patsy, how is she?" asked Richard not able to contain his curiosity any longer.

"Surviving. She's an amazing woman," replied Hussein as Charlotte rushed back.

"Sorry I've been ordered to drag you away, daddy's ready."

"I'll see you later Hussein. Don't go anywhere."

"Help yourself to Champagne." Charlotte pointed Hussein towards a large tray being ferried towards him at Charlotte's orders.

"I could get used to this," replied Hussein, helping himself to a glass and settling into a corner of the large room. He watched as Richard was hustled towards the front of the room, strategically placed next to Charlotte and her father.

Mr Hemmings held up a glass clinking on it for silence, which led to the hustle and bustle in the room dying down and everyone crowding round to listen intently.

"I'd like to thank you all for coming tonight which I'm sure you all agree has been a very long time coming, but thankfully we got there in the end. I would like to welcome Mr Templeton senior and his lovely wife whose hearts, I'm sure, swell with pride as they look on at their son Richard's achievements. We all know that for Richard this is just the beginning, but tonight isn't about making long speeches it's about the future and it gives me great pleasure to formally announce the appointment of the new Head of our Legal division for Formulie Enterprises and my future son-in-law Richard Templeton."

Hussein looked on as Richard made his way over to Randolph accompanied by applause, shaking his hand with gusto.

"Oh God this is slightly embarrassing" said Richard as the room responds with a controlled laughter. "This year has been an eventful one for me in more ways than one" he said as he glanced at Hussein. "And I would like to thank Randolph and the shareholders of Formulie Enterprises for taking a chance on an unknown entity such as myself and giving me this great opportunity, which I hope will allow me to take this extraordinary company to even greater heights. I've always lived my life dreaming and hoping that I could make a difference and with Pats ... perhaps with a woman like Charlotte by my side I can make that dream a reality."

Richard's words were acknowledged with a rapturous round of applause and Charlotte seemed oblivious to his gargantuan Freudian slip, hugging him tightly, followed by everyone around him. Richard accepted their congratulations, shaking various hands of people he did not know, but despite the accolades, he realised that only two people in that room knew what he yearned for. That was just a dream now, as she was a million miles away.

"Wow head of the legal division for one of the biggest corporations in the world and you also get the girl. You really have fallen on your feet, Templeton, but somehow that doesn't look like the face of a man who has it all."

"Is it wrong to have everything you want? Richard replied.

"No, but it's better to have everything you need" Hussein responded.

"Take care Hussein, and thank you," said Richard. Hussein looked on as Richard made his way into the crowd of unknown faces; joined by Charlotte, and his mind suddenly shot back to that night. He had broken all the rules, risked everything to save them and in the end, they saved him. He thought about what it would be like to be a normal man with a family of his own; a wife, children, but it was too late for the likes of him. He had done far too much damage to himself and others to ever stand a chance of forming a real relationship and if he did, the person would have to be very special; someone like Patsy, who had the ability to love and sacrifice everything for that love. He knew how much she must have been hurting, but she never attempted to contact Richard. She allowed him to live his life, be free to make his own choices, but sometimes, brilliant men can take the wrong road. He searched around the room until he found who he was looking for and as he excused his way through the crowd of people in his quest to meet Richard's father. He realised that saving Richard was now becoming a habit.

Chapter 32

❧

"Richard you really are a slob" said Martha Templeton as she picked up the discarded clothes scattered around Richard's room.

"Well if I'd known you and dad were going to descend upon me, I would have cleaned up. I still don't understand why you didn't stay at the hotel, surely it would have been a lot more comfortable."

"Because we don't get to spend enough time with our son as it is and I can imagine things will only get worse once you become an entrepreneurial mogul, so tonight we're squatting." Martha placed a pile of clothes in a basket. "I'm off to bed, and remember I've booked you for the entire day tomorrow, so no sneaking off." Martha disappeared into the bedroom.

John Templeton admired the view from Richard's flat in the heart of London.

"Can I interest you in a nightcap?" Richard asked.

"I think I could be persuaded." John replied, returning to the flat and closing the sliding door behind him. He settled down on the sofa while Richard poured him a large whisky.

"Smooth." said John, savouring the exquisite drink as it went down.

"Only the best for my old man."

They sat in silence for a while enjoying a rare moment together. As John took another sip, he studied his son who looked shattered after his busy day of endless meetings with shareholders and wedding planners. His eyes had emptiness behind them, despite the fact that he had the world at his feet.

"Your mother is extremely proud of you Richard."

"And what about you?"

"That goes without saying, but you've always made us proud. It doesn't take the likes of Randolph Hemmings to tell us you are an extraordinary young man ... So, you're giving up the hustle and bustle of court life. Funny I always thought you loved it."

"I do, but maybe it's time for a change."

"And such a drastic one, are you sure you've thought this through son?" John was careful in his choice of words.

"I've done nothing else dad, it's the best thing all round, new start, new life," replied Richard taking another drink, before making his way to the window overlooking the bright lights of London. "With any luck I can put this whole thing behind me, find a way to forget, move on."

"New beginnings, I'll drink to that" John took another sip.

"To new beginnings," replied Richard.

"So ... were you ever going to tell me about Patsy?"

"Bloody Hussein, how much did he tell you?"

"Only what happened that night, but don't worry, I haven't told your mother. She's worried enough. I knew there was something, the way you and the police closed ranks. Why in God's name didn't you tell me? All those months and I have to hear it from a complete stranger?"

"It wasn't my finest hour dad. It was a week of madness; sometimes I'm still not sure if it actually happened."

"Well I can understand why you kept it quiet, it wouldn't do to get involved with any scandal in relation to someone like that."

"Someone like what?" asked Richard, surprised at his father's unfamiliar callous attitude.

"I'm merely saying that it was good that you came to your senses before it was too late that's all. I mean thank God Charlotte never found out. If she had you could have lost everything that mattered, and those types of women are only out for what they can get."

"No dad, you don't understand it wasn't like that, she wasn't like that. I had never met anyone like her ... she's ... well she's amazing and a brilliant lawyer, who wasn't afraid to take me on when it counted. She's also funny and beautiful with a feistiness about her that I've never seen in a woman before. I could not have survived without her; she saved my life in more ways than one." John watched as he saw a passion return to his son that he had not seen for months and realised that he had only just scratched the surface of what his son had been hiding, but no matter how painful his words would be, he had no choice but to push the boundaries even further.

"I'm sorry Richard but I'm a little confused. I don't believe you cared for this Patsy at all."

"How can you say that?" said Richard beside himself.

"Because the Richard I know could never turn his back on someone he cared about and that's what you did isn't it?"

"I did what I thought was best. She's better off without me. I'm a liar and a cheat dad and she doesn't need someone like that in her life."

"And you've made this unilateral decision on behalf of the pair of you have you? Did you ever stop to consider what Patsy wanted, how she felt through all this?"

"What about how I felt! For weeks I lay in that bed not knowing what day it was and all I had for company was Arif rolling around and around in my head. I lost all sense of who I was and I wanted to be with Patsy I really did but she was ... she was..."

"A reminder of what happened ... and Charlotte?"

"She was there saying and doing all the right things. I honestly don't think I could have got through this without her. But Patsy ... Oh God, dad Patsy..." said Richard, finally allowing himself to break down in a sea of tears, collapsing into himself and losing all sense of control. John Templeton calmly rose and held his son, knowing that at last Richard was facing his demons.

"You were right dad; I couldn't have cared about her. I was a coward. I could not face her. I ran away and she needed me. She really needed me ... Arif he tried to..." said Richard as he continued to sob in his father's arms, not able to say the words aloud.

"Richard you went through a very traumatic experience; you nearly died."

"So did she."

"Yes, but you didn't; you both survived despite all the evil things that maniac did to you. You and Patsy survived." John pulled Richard away from him cupping his face gently in his hands. "But you've got to give yourself permission to live again, not out of a sense of duty to Charlotte or Randolph bloody Hemmings, but out of an obligation to yourself. You need to take your life back; be the Richard both your mother and I love, on your own terms. The sooner you do that, the sooner you'll heal."

"It's too late dad ... Charlotte ... the job."

"It's never too late. Now come on, pull yourself together; clean up and we we'll work this whole thing out." Richard felt like a boy again going to his father for all the answers and as they both talked into the early hours of that morning, with his mother sleeping soundly in the room next door, he realised that, like Patsy, he was truly blessed with an abundance of love that made him strong enough to do anything.

Chapter 33

❧

"Richard, what on earth are you doing here, I thought you were spending the day with your mother." Charlotte clasped a gold earring into place while remaining seated at her large dresser. Richard bent down giving her a quick peck on the cheek. "You could do with a shave." said Charlotte as she pulled away.

Richard sat on the edge of her bed, fidgeting in an attempt to get comfortable.

"You look like you haven't had a wink of sleep. Don't worry darling, I know exactly how you feel, it's all been a bit full on hasn't it? Oh, you'll never guess, mother has really surpassed herself this time; she only contacted the florists, changed my entire order without telling me. She is so stuffy, said my arrangements were a little understated, whatever that means. It has taken me ages to sort out the debacle and the day has barely begun. Not to mention the hangover I'm nursing from last night." Richard managed to raise a staggered smile, not taking in a word.

"Charlotte … we need to talk." He said.

"It will have to wait, I've got my final dress fitting in an hour and a million and one things to do, I am literally on the verge of a nervous breakdown." She continued.

"You're keen," said Isabella, standing at the door, carrying two glasses of Champagne. "God, you look how I feel." Isabella continued as she carried the drink over to Charlotte and laid it on the dresser table.

"I asked for a coffee."

"I thought about it and decided against it." Isabella collapsed on the Chaise Lounge, taking a leisurely sip from the champagne flute. "Richard, how rude of me, can I get you a glass?" Richard managed to muster a smile before refusing.

"Charlotte tells me you've asked your partner to be your best man." Richard could not help but notice the brief glance between the two women, showing a subtle look of disapproval.

"Rupert's a good friend, I would not dream of asking anyone else."

"But, he's a little ... eccentric don't you think and ... and slightly on the wrong side of fifty."

"Isabella, Rupert is Richard's choice and we need to respect that," said Charlotte applying the finishing touches to her make-up. Richard heard the insincerity behind her words. "God is that the time? We have got to go." Charlotte said, finished her Champagne and both women headed for the door. "Will you let yourself out Richard? Or better still, crash out here for a while."

"I said we need to talk."

"Can't it wait?"

"No," Richard insisted jumping to his feet "It's important. Isabella do you mind leaving us alone … please?"

"Of course, I'll wait downstairs," replied Isabella, looking a little worried as she closed the door behind her.

"Richard, what on earth is this about? You turn up here looking like death warmed up and…"

"Charlotte, for once in your life just stop … stop and listen. I really need you to listen."

Charlotte slowly sat down on the bed as Richard walked up and down trying to find the words. He had made a lucrative career weaving words in and out of one another to get what he wanted, yet now when it really mattered he was at a loss as to what to say.

"Richard for God's sake sit down you're making me nervous." Richard finally sat down, gently taking her hand, studying the flawless, smooth delicate skin, before eventually summoning up the courage.

"I can't do this." He whispered.

"What?"

"You … me … I can't do it." The words were out in the open, breathing fresh-air, bringing with them a wave of relief.

"Richard … darling, I completely understand what's happening here, you've been through so much, everything has roller-coasted so quickly, I can understand why it's left you a little confused."

"I am not confused Charlotte, in fact for the first time in my life I see everything clearly."

"Now I know you're being delusional. Richard you need to go home, get some rest unscramble that intricate brain of yours and I promise you we'll talk later." Said Charlotte getting up to leave, rejecting the information, treating it as a mere inconvenience.

"There's someone else..." Richard said suddenly, shocked at his revelation.

The declaration hit Charlotte, making it impossible to brush it aside. She had to think quickly. What should she do? Her first instinct was to fight back, regain control. She had worked hard to win Richard. For a while she felt like she was losing him, but after the trauma of Arif, he needed her; she had been with him at every step, nursing him back to health. In a morbid kind of way, Arif had given her a way back into Richard's wavering affection. They were the perfect couple, everyone said so. It was only right that they should be together. There was anger bubbling away inside her, building every second, yet, she had to maintain control. Under no circumstances would she allow it to take hold, because then she would surely lose everything she had laboured for; the status that came with being Mrs Richard Templeton and all that it would bring. Richard was the son her father never had, and she knew

Randolph Hemmings would guide and mould him into becoming one of the most influential men in the country. Charlotte had already picked out the perfect house, Maningale Ridge, just a few miles away from her parents. She fell in love with the beautiful dwelling, resting by a lake, from the moment she laid eyes on it; and now it was all hers, thanks to the generosity of her doting father. She had decided not to tell Richard about the extravagant gift until after the wedding, knowing him to be a proud man who would need a little persuading, so it made sense to wait. However, now her dream was unravelling and she had to find a way to salvage it. She wanted to know everything about her nemesis, but remained guarded in her questioning as she sat on the Chaise Lounge; she had the upper hand and needed to take full advantage of it.

"Who is she?" Charlotte asked calmly.

"She's no one you know, and before you ask, she does not work with me."

"That's something at least, are you still seeing her?"

"No, I haven't seen her in months."

"Was it serious?"

"Six days, it lasted precisely six days." As Charlotte saw the hurt behind Richard's eyes, she knew those six days were a lifetime to him. Who was this bitch, this rival, presuming to come into her life and take what did not belong to her? The biggest question of all sat on the tip of her tongue; nonetheless, she refused to ask it, knowing what his answer would be. Did he love the insignificant spec that had intruded upon her? Yet, Charlotte's mother taught her long ago a woman needs more than love to keep her in the lavish lifestyle she deserves. She also needs wit, an agility of the mind to hook her prey. Her mother had done it with her father and now history was somehow repeating itself, and even though Charlotte hated Richard for what he had done, she was not about to release him. She was a beautiful woman with the world at her feet and now would be the perfect time to put that to good use. Removing her jacket, she approached Richard, sitting closely by him on the bed.

"It seems to me, this indiscretion on your part was over before it began, would you agree?" Charlotte began to brush her fingers through Richard's hair. Richard did not answer, instead simply shook his exhausted head in agreement. "Then I think the only logical thing to do is draw a line under it." Richard suddenly pulled back, stunned, but Charlotte did not let go, pulling him back towards her, cupping his face in her hands. "Darling, I would be the first to admit, before this awful episode with that monster happened, you and I were drifting apart. I have to accept that I was not as supportive as I could have been regarding your legal career. But, I promise you things will be different now, over the last few months you and I have grown closer than ever. We have a bright, wonderful future ahead of us; a brand new start and I am not about to let anything get in the way of that. I can see how upset you are about all this and I appreciate that you have decided to be honest with me. I love you Richard and do not want to lose you. Because of that, I am prepared to be the bigger person, wipe the slate clean, start afresh. As of now, doing what we do best, make up in the only way we know how." Charlotte made her way over to the dresser drawer, she removed the small package that she unwrapped before returning to Richard and pulling at his trousers, forcing her hand down his front, making him stand erect, as she kissed him passionately, before manoeuvring herself on top of him, tugging her underwear away, not giving him a chance as she jammed him inside her. They rocked in perpetual motion and although enjoying the experience, Richard felt dazed, drugged even. It was as if he was in a maze and was searching for a way out.

"This is what you want. You see Richard, we are good together, we are so good together. Doesn't that feel good, don't I feel good?" Charlotte hissed in his ear, but this was not what he came here to do, this was not what he wanted. He began to fight, take a hold of his senses, detach himself from the physical pleasure. Charlotte writhed on top of him, pushing him deeper and deeper inside her and it was at that moment he senses suddenly clicked back into place.

"No, this is wrong, this is all wrong," said Richard finally managing to push Charlotte away and off him.

They both lay on the bed breathing heavily, before Richard slowly rose and pulled up his trousers.

"I don't want this Charlotte; I don't want any of it."

Charlotte got up, composing herself; it was time to show her claws "Don't be ridiculous, you would not have any of this if it wasn't for me. Do you really think my father would have anything to do with you if I am not part of the package? You don't get one without the other."

"Jesus?" said Richard

"Don't look so shocked Richard; you should know by now, I would do anything to get what I want!"

"Good bye Charlotte," Richard grabbed his jacket and headed out the door.

"Who do you think you are? You can't walk away from me! No one walks away from me!" Charlotte yelled, storming after Richard down the stairs where Isabella was waiting, understandably very confused.

"What on earth is going on?" asked Isabella.

"I'm finishing with him. Take a look, Isabella, at a treacherous, cheating bastard. Richard bloody Templeton is nothing but a fake, a boring legalistic pen pusher and I am well rid of him. All this time he was only using me to get to my father's company, he never cared about me, he never cared about any of us."

Although regretful for the pain he had caused, Richard realised that in the end, for Charlotte, it came down to appearances, and how she looked to society and her friends. He allowed her to spin her yarn, it was easier that way and he owed her that much. However, one thing he did do was ensure Patsy's name was kept out of it, as he had no wish to subject her to any more pain.

* * *

Unpopularity was an unusual experience for Richard. Being shunned and whispered about was not enjoyable. He was no longer the blue-eyed boy, with Randolph Hemmings making it clear that there was no place in his company for someone who could treat his daughter in such a callous manner. Telling him what a fool, he had been, throwing such a promising career away. Even though he had no intention of working for Randolph, it was still a difficult pill to swallow. Yet, Richard had a niggling feeling that no matter how hard he tried, he would have lost all sense of independence under the powerful mogul, because the Randolph Hemmings' of this world did not get to where they were by loosening the reins, and Richard had never been good at living in someone else's shadow.

Rupert was of course ecstatic at Richard's return to the fold, "You do realise I've lost the entire female clientele contingency; I relied on your good looks to bring in the punters. I am thankful that the status quo is now firmly back in its rightful place." It was not exactly

PC, but Richard was glad that at least here, nothing had changed. Even Maggie welcomed him back with an out of the norm hearty hug; making it clear to him, he was back where he belonged.

Yet, the most difficult task still lay ahead of him, with everything else being a walk in the park in comparison. Richard watched as Joyce left her offices accompanied by two colleagues and plucked up the courage to leave the safety of his car, putting their last meeting firmly to the back of his mind. He was not surprised to see Joyce's face drop as he made his way across the busy street, but despite her look of disdain he continued until they were face to face. It was difficult to know what to say so he decided that it would be best to cut straight to the chase.

"Hello Joyce, I know I'm the last person you want to see, but the thing is I need your help."

Chapter 34

꙲

"Anna for the last time I am not going to Magaluf."
Anna and I made our way up the stairs towards my flat,
loaded down with various bags from the retail therapy
that Anna convinced me I needed.

"Pats we'd have a wicked time; sun, sea and Sangria.
I'm telling you it would be great! Just picture it, all
those bronzed biceps."

"Yeah staggering along the strip binge drinking
themselves into oblivion."

"When in Rome" replied Anna as I stopped outside
my door fiddling for my keys amongst the plethora of
rubbish hidden in the far corners of my bag.

"I've always wanted to go to Venice, it looks so
beautiful there."

"You're on your own on that one."

Suddenly my mobile went off and I struggled to find
it. "I swear one day I am going to give this bag a good
clear out ... Hello ... Oh hello Mr Rawlings what can
I do for you? ... Right ... Ok ... But I finished the report
yesterday ... what additional information? ... Well this

is the first I'm hearing about that, can't anybody else do it? ... I know there's a deadline Mr Rawlings ... But that would mean working over the weekend." I tried my best to ignore Anna's frantic waves of disapproval. "I am sorry Mr Rawlings, but I'm afraid I can't do that ... Why? ... Because I have a life Mr Rawlings and I intend to spend the weekend with my family, as well as plan a well-deserved holiday with a very long suffering friend." Before Mr Rawlings could respond, I ended the call.

"Ok, can you please tell me what you've done with my friend Patsy Cunningham?"

"Very funny," I continued searching in my bag until I found my keys, and clumsily pinned the bags against the door with my legs to stop them from flying everywhere. I pushed the door open with my back, immediately discarding the load in the hallway.

"Fancy a glass of wine?" I asked as I made my way to the kitchen. I suddenly stopped dead in my tracks as I found Richard standing in my front room. It had been exactly three months, five days and six hours since I had seen him and today was the first morning I had not thought about him, giving a glimmer of hope that maybe, finally, I was beginning to move on with my life. Yet, I should have known Richard, being Richard, would not allow that to happen. He lulled me into a false sense of security only to spring back into my life when I least expected it.

"Now before you kick off Patsy, I want you to hear him out," said Joyce, surfacing from my kitchen carrying two cups of tea, which she gently placed on the living room table. "I know that you'll probably never forgive me but I had no choice, you need closure Patsy. You need to move on with your life and that can never happen, until the two of you have it out in the open. I am under no illusions about this man having a way with words, but you are my priority in all this and I am so worried about you. I know you are saying and doing all the right things, but I know you're not happy."

"She's right Pats," said Anna, which made it clear to me that they had cooked this up between them.

I had planned this moment in my mind for so long; how I would act, what I would say and all of it was bog standard stuff for someone who had been hurt, rejected. I wanted to tell him that he was a two-timing cheat who had no right to be in my life, who left me to cope with persistent nightmares, sleepless nights as well as the fear of seeing Arif around every corner coupled with the guilt and shame of ending his life. I had planned to tell him that he had hurt me, that I hated him for it. However, things never go the way you plan, no matter how much thought you put into it, and seeing a distressed and clearly worn out Richard standing in front of me with eyes darkened by tiredness and guilt somehow put my own feelings into perspective.

"Patsy, are you listening to me?" Joyce's voice faded in and out whilst Richard and I remained spellbound by one another.

"How are you?" Richard asked.

"I'm getting there" I replied "And you?"

"I've been better," responded Richard. Joyce and Anna must have left because I realised we were suddenly alone. I don't know how long we stood there, maybe it was half an hour maybe more but I do know that it was me who took the first step towards him as I watched the tear fall down his face.

"I need to know that you forgive me" Richard whispered "for deceiving you, for letting all this happen."

"We're both to blame. We knew what we were doing and we have paid for that. I think that the only way we are going to get through this is to start forgiving ourselves."

"So much has happened Patsy. I've made so many mistakes. In trying not to let anybody down, I've only ended up hurting everyone. I learnt more about myself in that one week with you than I had with anyone in my life. I cannot remember ever being so happy."

"What about Charlotte?" Lawyers have a golden rule when cross-examining; if you do not know the answer to a question, you should never ask it, but today even though I did not know the answer, I had to ask.

"Charlotte and I are over. In fact I don't think we ever really began."

At that moment, I knew that I was free. Free to do what I had wanted to do from the moment I saw him again. I knew Richard and I needed to heal and I could not think of a better way than this. I gently took his hand and led him into the bedroom closing the door behind us and, for the first time in three long months, we both had a restful, peaceful sleep.

Chapter 35

"I can't believe we just did that." I said looking at Richard shell-shocked.

"Well you know what they say Pats, there's a first time for everything. Are you ready?" asked Richard, tightly holding my hand as always, guiding the way.

"As I'll ever be," I said, still not quite taking in what was actually happening.

We both watched as the large doors opened and the room full of guests rose to their feet and the master of ceremonies led the way.

"Ladies and Gentlemen it gives me great pleasure to introduce to you, for the first time, Mr and Mrs Richard Templeton."

Breath. Patsy, breath…

End